Wolf Shield

Guardians of Chaos 1

C.D. Gorri

Wolf Shield

Guardians of Chaos Book 1
by C.D. Gorri
Edited by BookNookNuts
Copyright 2020, 2022 C.D. Gorri, NJ

*To all the freethinkers and the people not afraid to get messy, keep
on creating, the world needs you.*
Xoxo,
C.D.

*STOP! Before you go, sign up for my newsletter and get the latest
on my releases, giveaways, freebies and more:*
www.cdgorri.com/newsletter/newsletter

Description

She's a normal caught in a supernatural war, and he's the only man who can save her.

Hudson Stormwolfe is a Guardian of Chaos. His order is tasked with keeping magic free to ensure the flourishment of supernaturals through innovative thought and creativity without fear of persecution.

But there are those who wish to put a cap on freedom. A group called the Loyalists have sworn themselves enemies of the Guardians and all they stand for. They want the power to control all magic.

Fergie McAndrews is a typical normal with an atypical obsession for shoes. Her no nonsense attitude has gotten her in trouble with previous employers, but she is determined to make this new job work. She even goes so far as to put in overtime.

But what was with the creepy green goons who wanted to take a bite out of the pleasantly plump female? Tossed into a fight between supernaturals, the human woman is about to get got until he steps in.

Storm can't help but be drawn to the curvy female. Her voice, her scent, her smile all call to his inner Wolf. Ready or not, this Guardian has found his fated mate, but can he save the fiery redhead from harm and convince her she belongs to him?

Storm will do anything to claim his mate, even promise to keep her in the ridiculously expensive shoes she favors.

Guardians of Chaos Pledge

I am the watcher in the storm.
I am the iron shield.
I protect against those who seek to control the wild
nature of magic.
I am the guardian of chaos.
To thrive, we must be free.
From chaos comes creation.

Prologue

"Why are we traipsing through the fucking swamp to meet your so-called contact, Fur?" Hudson Stormwolfe, or Storm as he was known, growled at his friend and fellow Guardian, "a goddamn coffee shop wouldn't do?"

The Horse Shifter snorted as Storm stepped in a hole cursing quietly as a trickle of slimy sludge slipped inside his once clean steel-toed boots.

"Oh, you are going to scrape these clean," he shot at Furio.

"Dude, just watch your step," Furio retorted making a show of how easily his long legs ate up the muddy landscape.

Fuck him, snarled Storm's Wolf. Trudging

through the muck was not his animal's idea of a good time. Give him a dense, clean forest any day. Storm only agreed to accompany Furio because Kingston told him to go.

Their leader could be a hard ass at times, but no one fucked with the Dragon Shifter just lately. Not because they were afraid, but for other reasons. Losing one's mate could really fuck a guy up inside. Besides, Storm had liked Neela, may she rest in peace for eternity.

Damn the Loyalists. Those bastards were nothing more than terrorists and fanatics attacking supernatural creatures and hoarding magic for their own nefarious purposes. They wanted to control and siphon out the one thing every supernatural needed to live with their leaders as the gatekeepers. That thing was of course magic itself.

Loyalists believed that common folk had no business accessing magic. They wanted to keep it for the elite, the wealthy, and basically anyone who did what they said. They were nothing more than pirates and madmen as far as Storm was concerned.

They had been around for nearly as long as the Guardians of Chaos. Storm was proud to call himself a Guardian. He was more than able and willing to do his part to ensure freedom for all supernatural-kind.

Even after all this time, those bastards still failed to gain the momentum necessary to achieve their goals. Their terroristic acts were the stuff of nightmares. Especially this latest attack on the Guardians' leader. The heinous crime was without precedent.

It still left a bad taste in Storm's mouth. He gritted his teeth as his mind still tried to take in the fact she was gone. Neela Baldric, the beloved mate of their once fearless leader, was brutally attacked while on her way to the supermarket.

The gentlewoman was a rare and precious creature and was mated to his superior, Kingston Baldric, for many years. She'd only just succumbed to her wounds a few months ago, leaving all of them bereft of her company, but none so much as Kingston.

"We all miss her, bro," Furio said, and Storm realized he'd been projecting.

Fuck. He hated it when he did that. Though truthfully, it wouldn't have mattered. Furio felt her loss as well. Everyone in Kingston's group of Guardians felt the loss keenly.

These kinds of terroristic acts were the new tool the Loyalists used to persuade mainstream paranormal society to their way of thinking. Blackmail, bribery, murder, mayhem, all elements of destruction that this so-called law-abiding organization stooped to in order to fulfill their aims.

Not on his watch, Storm vowed to himself. It was his job and that of all the Guardians to stop those bastards and ensure freedom for their kind.

"Sorry," Storm muttered, "still, we had to meet in a fucking swamp, Furio?"

"What swamp, bro? We're in Secaucus," Furio opened his arms wide and gestured to the thick, musty smelling wetland they were currently stalking through.

It was just a little past ten o'clock at night, but summer in the Garden State meant hot and sticky. Especially in that small portion of undeveloped marshlands. Storm growled when his foot sank yet again, ankle-deep, into another muddy hole.

Goddamn it, he grimaced, and slapped his friend in the back of the head. Then he counted to three like he'd been told to do by another of their own, Egros, a male Witch who thought the Wolf Shifter would have better control if he could simply manage his anger.

Yeah. Right. The hell with counting. He was going to kick Furio's ass when they were done here.

"Half the fucking state is a swamp," Storm

growled, shaking the muck off his foot, "I thought you were born here?"

"I was. Born and bred in Hoboken, *cumpy*."

"What?"

"Nothin' man, just some local slang from when I was a kid. Anyway, you're shittin' me right, New Jersey isn't a swamp," snorted the Stallion Shifter.

Storm rolled his eyes and blew out a breath. What was he going to do with this guy? Thirty years as a Guardian, and Furio was still a rookie to Storm, who'd spoke his vows over a hundred years ago this past April.

As a Wolf Shifter, he had a longer than average life expectancy, which had only increased when he'd pledged his allegiance to serve all the supernatural creatures living on this planet as a Guardian. He'd fought too many battles to count, but the work was meaningful. Protecting freedom always was.

It had been the same for his grandfather, who'd raised him just outside the boundaries of the Pack where his father still ruled as Alpha. His older brother was the heir which usually meant younger brothers were ousted or had to challenge for positions in the Pack. Rather than stay and fight for his dominance in the place of his birth, he'd left.

Storm respected tradition, but he had had a

higher calling to serve. The Guardians of Chaos were an elite order of supernaturals. The higher ups did not want it said they were showing favoritism to any specific Pack, Clan, Coven or what have you, so they composed each unit of a mix of *supes*. It took years to build the kind of team Storm was a part of.

Furio might be considered new, but he was still one of them. So fine, maybe Storm wouldn't kick his ass outright, but he could best him in training. That would satisfy both his Wolf and human sides.

"Did you hear Kingston has a meeting with the Assembly next week to discuss Neela's passing?" Furio spoke in a low voice, but with his supernaturally enhanced senses, Storm heard him just fine.

"I did. The Assembly, are all former Guardians, they will understand Kingston's loss and will likely support his call to mount a hunt for the Loyalist who'd ordered the hit," Storm responded.

"We're not Enforcers, Storm. Their job is to police the paranormal peoples of the earth, not ours. Guardians of Chaos don't promote actual chaos, right?" asked Furio, and he was right to a point.

"Look, we are called Guardians of Chaos, because from chaos, aka freedom, comes creativity. If we lose that, we perish. A Guardian is the ultimate protector of free thought, and therefore, the champion of creation itself. Neela was a cherished female and Kingston's to protect and to avenge. We might not understand what it is like to be mated, Furio, but he has rights and this did happen because of our war," Storm responded.

"All for magic? Neela was killed so the Loyalists could control magic? How would that even happen?"

"No, she was killed to break us. Without our leader, the Loyalists hope to win whatever scheme they are hatching and believe me, they are always plotting something. Whoever controls magic, controls us all," he grunted.

The way Storm understood it, magic was a finite thing, like ore, it was distributed organically, used, and recycled by each supernatural group as needed. The ancient ones, gods, goddesses, or what have you created magic out of chaos for each paranormal species to grow and take shape.

"What would they do, if they had it all?" Furio asked.

"What's with all the fucking questions?" growled Storm.

It was not for any one of them to control the others' usage of this gift. It went against their very nature as magical creatures.

Storm understood this. It was why he'd never

looked back after leaving the Black Moon Pack to follow in his grandfather's footsteps. With his father still ruling and his brother as heir, his life there would have been difficult to say the least.

He was too dominant. More so than his old man, yet the tradition dictated that the second son could not be Alpha.

Leaving was his only option, and his grandfather had ensured that he had all the knowledge he needed before his time came. Storm had joined the crusade against those who sought to rule over the entire supernatural world before he was old enough to vote. He knew his duty was no longer to Pack, but to his band of Guardians.

Which was why he was wading through the last thick patch of swampland left undeveloped in Secaucus, New Jersey, home of the best outlet shopping this side of the Hudson River for which he was named, at the behest of one of his own.

Fucking Furio.

"Sorry, *cump*, talking helps pass the time. Anyway, my CI prefers to be away from prying eyes, you know he's part Goblin, and more than a little skittish."

"Yeah, well, what news does he have, anyway?"

"He thinks he found the Loyalists' new headquarters. It was too good a tip to pass up. He's supposed to have the GPS coordinates for me tonight."

"Shit. That is important. But he couldn't have texted them?"

"Nah," Furio shook his head, causing his long hair, which was bound in a leather thong to sway side to side, mimicking that of his shifted form.

He stopped to touch one of the long overgrown cattails they'd passed, and Storm stilled in his tracks, wondering if he heard something. Like a woman breathing or humming or something. But how could that be? They were in the middle of nowhere. Furio dropped the cattail and turned toward the soft, and admittedly pleasant, vocals.

"Hey, you hear that?" Furio asked.

Storm raised his hand to quiet the other man. His Wolf was at full attention. A warm breeze blew in their direction, and he breathed it in deep siphoning through the various layers, hoping to identify whatever made that sound.

Along with the heavy scent of the dense and decaying vegetation, came another, lighter, much more pleasant fragrance. It sifted through Storm's highly acute olfactory system, teasing and tempting his senses. Whatever it was, Storm wanted more.

His Wolf's ears worked to zero in on the source of both the sounds and the tantalizing fragrance that seemed too soft, too fine for the misty marshlands of Secaucus, New Jersey.

"It's like brown sugar and marzipan," he murmured as the sweet fragrance danced across his senses, like something out of a dream.

"What?" laughed Furio, but he ignored the Stallion.

He knew better than to go traipsing off after a phantom scent, but there was something about it. Something all too tempting and familiar. Storm's Wolf perked up. He growled low and deep as he took in another breath.

That scent, that crazy good scent, was like a shock to the system, but not necessarily unpleasant. More like an awakening. Storm noticed the Stallion Shifter walking through the thicket towards that divine fragrance, and the Wolf inside of him snarled.

"What the fuck, *cump*?" Furio asked.

Storm shook his head. What the fuck was wrong with him? Furio was his friend and fellow Guardian.

It didn't matter. It upset the Wolf. Storm shook his head and tried to silence the beast, but his animal was insistent. He needed to beat his friend to the source of that heavenly scent.

"Shit," he growled.

He hurried past the Stallion, using his superior height to gain the advantage, despite Furio's better speed. The Stallion couldn't beat him there. Storm would not allow it. He leapt over fallen trees and shrubs, avoiding the holes that had gotten him twice already in the deceptively soft, wet earth, until he reached the edge of what seemed to be a parking lot.

The heavy breathing coming from behind him told the Wolf that Furio had managed to keep pace, but the Stallion needed to hit the gym more if he was out of breath. It was shameful for a Guardian to be so easily exhausted. Then again, when had he ever beaten the Horse Shifter in a race?

"Damn, Storm, I never saw you run so fast," he huffed and Storm blinked in surprise, "shit, if I'd have known this lot was so close, I wouldn't have made us park behind the stadium and walk," the Stallion sucked in air greedily.

"Shhh," Storm held up his hand for silence.

His Wolf's enhanced vision allowed him to make out the details of the scene before him. They were just outside the fenced in parking lot of some kind of building. There was a municipal sign hanging up not too far away.

It was late at night, so it wasn't the courthouse,

and there were no cop cars parked outside, so it wasn't a police station either. He looked around for any other indication of what the older cement building was. Ah, another dented sign.

"It's a library," Furio whispered.

"I see that," Storm growled.

He was angry and on edge, and he had no fucking idea why. His entire body vibrated with energy. He was not nervous, just impatient, he realized. That was odd, too.

What could he possibly be waiting for here? His Wolf dripped saliva from his fangs as he waited in that metaphysical plane where he rested until Storm called to him. He tried to consider what led him there, but all coherent thought fled his brain the second *she* came into view.

The strange woman was all the way on the other end of the tiny parking lot. A tall security fence and a good fifty feet of black asphalt stood between the female and the place where the two Guardians lurked, but Storm could still make out every detail of the stunning creature.

"She's a little round, but I always did like a girl with some cushion for the pushin'," Furio elbowed him jokingly, but his words enraged Storm.

The Wolf inside of him snarled and growled and

before he could stop himself, he had Furio by the collar of his shirt. He'd lifted the Stallion a good foot off the ground before shock had him dropping his friend.

"The fuck?" Furio choked and rubbed his bruised neck.

Storm ignored him, eyes glued to the woman in the ankle-length skirt and short-sleeved blouse. She wore shiny red shoes with high spindle-like heels. *Stilettos*, he thought, and for the first time he understood why they were called that.

They might not be good for running, but the long, skinny heels could pierce a man's heart just like the stealthy blade someone named them after. As it was, he more than appreciated the way the shiny red heels lengthened her legs and caused her hips to sway seductively in the yellowish glow of the streetlights.

Her hair was pulled back in a loose bun. She'd obviously tried to tame her fiery red locks, but curls still fell around her lovely face. Storm observed the subtle highlights and lowlights in her hair color even in the diminished light, noting with pleasure her eyelashes held the same coppery tinge.

So, she was a natural redhead. Good. He did not like artificial things. Unlike most redheads who leaned towards fair-skinned, this beautiful woman had a healthy bronze glow to her. Her whiskey brown eyes were large and bright in the darkness.

He appreciated her plump pink lips, straight nose, and stubborn little chin. She was a knockout. The most gorgeous creature he'd ever laid eyes on.

Storm was thunderstruck. He watched her innocently sashay across the otherwise deserted parking lot to a beat up looking pick-up truck.

Hmm. Odd car choice, he thought.

That was all he had time to think as three men crept out of the shadows and circled the tiny female. Blood rushed through his being and he couldn't make out what was being said.

Whatever it was, didn't matter. One of them dared grab her arm and tossed her purse aside. Storm's fangs lengthened and claws popped free of his nails. The sound of her scream woke something furious inside of him. His entire body trembled with the strength of his fury. He needed to get to her. Now. There was no time to lose.

"Uh, what is that?" Furio tapped his shoulder and Storm turned and snarled.

His friend pointed down. Storm looked and took a step back in surprise. His palms were glowing. Small blue lights were circling both hands. His feet and legs were covered in what looked like shadowy black smoke billowing skywards. It was magic. He knew that much. It didn't hurt, but he'd never felt it before.

"Holy shit, Storm! Do you know what this means?"

Then it hit him. The reason for all the sudden changes. He turned to Furio and growled one word.

"Mine."

His female shrieked and hit the ground, and the Wolf inside him howled in fury.

Protect, the Wolf demanded.

He barely blinked his eyes, then he was directly in front of the female. It was like he'd moved through time and space. Storm appeared in front of her, shielding her from the soon-to-be-dead men who dared touch what was his.

He lifted his lip and snarled at the three assholes. It was nothing more than legend, he'd always thought. A fairy tale to keep younger *supes* from leaving the order. But he might have to change his mind.

He lifted his fists, still glowing with blue magic, and slammed it into the face of the first one of the three to launch an attack against him. Sparks flew, as did the assailant's teeth.

"What are you waiting for," Storm said to the other two.

He smiled wickedly. Looked like even Shifter fairy tales were true sometimes. It was rumored that the Guardians were blessed by the Fates that upon finding their true mates they would receive certain magical benefits to promote honoring their vows till death.

Stronger together, those were the words etched inside the doorway of the Keep. Now Storm finally understood their meaning.

"Mine," he looked down into startled butter-scotch eyes.

He knew without doubt; the woman was his mate, and he would shield her from harm.

Always.

Chapter One

What a day! Fergie McAndrews headed towards the pick-up truck she'd borrowed from her roommate for work that morning.

Of course, the thirty-thousand dollar certified used luxury car she'd splurged on earlier in the year was in the shop. Again.

Just another in a long line of bad decisions. After leaving a perfectly good job for a startup company, she was laid off three weeks ago and had to borrow money from her parents to pay rent. Wasn't that humiliating?

"This is the last time, Ferg," her step-monster had said after she'd Venmo'd the money to her.

God forbid the mechanic call and tell her the car

was ready. She wouldn't be able to pick it up for another week. That was when she got her first paycheck from her newest gig at L-Corp. Not a startup, but an older company with new offices in Bayonne, which was only a half-hour commute.

But to commute, you needed a car. Fergie had no choice but to borrow the old pick-up from her best friend and roommate, Jessenia Banks. It wasn't like she needed the truck. She worked from home these days. Besides, Fergie promised to fill it up and have it washed.

She huffed out a breath. It'd been a really long day. A crappy one too. Fergie wanted to love her new job. Really, she did. But so far, it was the pits. If Fergie wanted to be a librarian, she would've been one.

Research was her jam. Well, when it was interesting. She had a knack for sniffing out information and compiling easy-to-read spreadsheets and timelines. It wasn't the hard work that annoyed her. Her complaint was the content. The actual stuff her new boss had her looking up. It was beyond boring.

Why an enormous conglomerate like L-Corp needed old land surveys, cross-referenced with newspaper reports on accidents, crimes, etcetera. She had no idea. She'd been at it for weeks now. So far, she'd researched six locations given via GPS coordinates across Hudson County. Her new boss wanted everything, every little insignificant piece of information she could dig up.

That was the easy part. It was the hassle of the actual job that really made her want to give up. Every day she had to drive to Bayonne to pick up her work laptop she'd dropped off the night before with all of that day's findings. Every single night they wiped her computer clean.

Like she was going to run away with the secrets of what happened on 2nd and Washington sixty-years ago. Can you say paranoid? Ugh.

Fergie had always looked forward to working for a huge global company. It was supposed to be her ticket out of the Garden State. Travelling the globe, seeing new thi. Butngs, visiting far-off places was always a secret dream of hers. Well, that, and having her own walk-in closet full of gorgeous designer shoes.

Best secret dream evah! In her opinion, anyway. What woman didn't love shoes? Fergie hummed as she daydreamed about rows and rows of Blahnik's, Jimmy Choo's, Garavani's, Ferragamo's, and her personal favorites, Louboutin's on every shelf!

Don't judge. Fergie wasn't shallow, she just liked

pretty things. Haters gonna hate. But every time she ran across a thrift or second-chance store, she'd search high and low to see what they had. That was how she'd scored the pumps on her feet.

They made her feel good about herself. Being five-foot two-inches short with more curves than a racetrack, Fergie had had more than her fair share of self-esteem issues growing up. Alright, so she was chubby. She could admit that proudly now.

If everyone looked the same, the world would be one boring as hell place. Fergie liked herself perfectly fine these days, in spite of all the times her step-monster tried to make her diet growing up. So she liked food and shoes. Big deal.

She worked hard to feed and clothe herself, so as far as she was concerned, no one had a right to comment. So what if she wanted some excitement in her life? Fergie was aware she was better off than most, but what was wrong with having goals?

She'd spent a lot of time thinking about how a woman like her could have an adventure. Travelling was the only thing she could think of. Of course, she'd been hoping this job would be the answer to that. Even travelling for work was better than being stuck.

Sigh.

So far, her plans had fallen flat, but hey, at least she was earning a paycheck. Her new boss, Mr. Offner, might be a strange man, but he signed her checks, and that was enough for now. Fergie had never seen more than a glimpse of him. All of her instructions usually came via email.

Most of the time she was able to compile her research quickly, then she'd head back to the office to organize it into neat little spreadsheets, and finally, she'd hand it all in with her laptop. But not today.

Mr. Offner sent her an email detailing everything she could dig up on one of the oldest places on record in the county. Of course, land surveys that old, along with police reports, newspaper articles, deeds, and sales records were nowhere she could easily access them.

After wasting hours at both the court house and municipal building, Fergie had been directed to the *second* public library. Apparently anything over a hundred years old was filed away in the godforsaken place. She'd been shocked to find an entire room filled with musty old archives. And wouldn't you know it, there was no cell service and no internet access. Plus, their phone lines were down. She'd had to photograph each page using her cell. When she got home later, she would send those photos like a fax to her boss along with her spreadsheet. If she could manage that before collapsing into bed.

Boy, was she tired! She should've gone home ages ago, but Fergie was no quitter. Only once did she skip out of the library to grab a venti mocha latte with skim. She so loved curbside delivery!

Then she'd headed back over to the Second Free Public Library down on Paterson Plank Road. Properly caffeinated, she'd hunkered down and got to doing more of the work she was being paid to do.

Why the old building was called the second library was a mystery to her. One she didn't really care about, so, whatever.

Her job was to gather all the info she could on some old, currently vacant, piece of land formerly owned by Abel Smith. Mr. Offner, and therefore L-Corp, wanted every scrap of info she could muster up on the land which included a burial plot that had its own creepy folklore surrounding it.

Not her concern, she told herself, though some stories made the hair on the back of her neck stand on end. The land was bisected by Secaucus road and was actually not too far from the very library where she now found herself.

Fergie stopped walking and scolded herself for behaving like a schoolgirl. She was a professional adult woman, for Pete's sake! Her dedication to finding out miniscule details had earned her a GPA of 3.96 in college, and she'd taken that work ethic and experience with her wherever she went after graduating.

Fairy tales and campfire stories aside, she would give all the information to Mr. Offner tomorrow. She might not have the job of her dreams, but at least she could pay her bills. For now, she'd settle for that.

"Two hours to find the musty old ledger," she mumbled aloud while digging for the keys.

It was dark out and she was alone. That always made her nervous. Talking out loud helped calm her irrational fears. Adult or not, nobody liked being alone in a dark, creepy parking lot in the middle of the night. At least, Fergie didn't.

She'd prefer being back inside that horrible little room, reading the small handwritten columns in those old ledgers. And that had been no picnic either. After begging the nerdy little clerk to let her stay late, promising to lock up, she'd spent a total of six hours in the awful place. It was a wonder her eyes still worked.

She blew out a breath. Where the heck were the truck keys? She grabbed her cell phone. Of course, she still had zero bars, so no service, but oh well, at least she could use it as a flashlight. Just what she wanted from a nine-hundred dollar smart phone. Thank God they had monthly payment plans.

"Stupid piece of junk," Fergie blew out a breath and rummaged through her purse.

It was already after ten. She could probably wait till morning to bring her computer back to the office. She didn't use it anyway. All her info was on her phone. Besides, right then, all she wanted was sleep.

Fergie dropped the phone back in her bag. She'd located the keys and hummed to herself as she headed towards her borrowed truck. Her new scanning app was really something. She would use it as soon as she woke up and email her boss.

Mr. Offner was sure to be impressed with it. The software allowed her to convert images, like the ones she took of the ledgers and hand-drawn maps, into readable and printable PDFs. She wanted to make a good impression, and who knows, maybe she could land a promotion that would get her out of all this scut work.

One thing she knew for certain, Fergie could live the whole rest of her life and never step foot in that creepy ass parking lot or the old second library again. Who thought it was a good idea to put this place all the way on the edge of town?

There wasn't a drive thru or gas station anywhere in the vicinity. Just an old patch of marshland, which now that she thought of it, meant tons of creepy crawlies. Fergie loved animals, but not the kind that lived there. Rats, snakes, spiders, and bird-sized mosquitos.

Ew. She shivered and picked up the pace. It had been hot all day, and the local vegetation stunk something awful. She swatted away one huge blood-sucking fiend of an insect and crinkled her nose.

How Fergie could still smell the stink of the swamp with her allergies was beyond her? Speaking of which, it was way past the time she normally took her meds. She stopped walking again and started to dig through her pocketbook for her regularly prescribed allergy meds. If she didn't take them at the same time every night, they didn't work. A noise brought her head up, and she turned around fast.

"Hello, anyone there?" she questioned the dimly lit parking lot, feeling a tad foolish for doing so.

Too many scary movies, she scolded herself. She bent her head to check for the pills once more when the sound returned. Except this time it was directly behind her, making her jump.

Fergie whirled around and came face to face with three monstrously tall men. Her would-be assailants were all huge compared to her, even with heels on. She couldn't really make out their faces in the dim streetlights, but what she could see made her shudder.

Was it possible for three men to all have the same scale-like scars on their skin? Wait, was their skin green?

"Hello yourself," one of the men said, "*what'sssss* in the bag?"

"Holy shit," Fergie gasped in horror.

The speaker opened his mouth, and she swore she saw a row of needlelike teeth and a long, forked tongue poking out.

What the fucking fuck? Fergie swallowed. Hard.

Chapter Two

Before she could think to run or move at all, the strange-looking man ripped her purse right out of her hands and tossed it on the ground behind him.

Shit. Her keys were still inside the bag. Sure she knew there was always a chance of violence happening to a woman alone at night, she'd even read about an increase in muggings in town, but she'd never imagined it could happen to her.

She straightened her back, Fergie wasn't about to play the victim. Not for anyone. Cupping her hand around the lipstick tube she'd managed to grab, she addressed the would-be muggers as she'd been taught in her self-defense class back when she was still in school.

"Look, just take the bag, and leave me alone," she said in a firm voice.

"Well, now boys, we got *oursssselves* a *feissssty* one," the largest attacker hissed his words.

Fergie's eyes darted from one to the next. This was so not going to end in her favor. She squeezed the tube of lipstick, holding it as if it were a lifeline. Fergie was in trouble and she knew it.

Oh well, she *might as well go down swinging*. Fergie lifted her hand around the tube of lipstick in a defensive position.

"Stand back! I've got pepper spray!" she lied, and the three of them laughed.

Rude! She narrowed her eyes at the three hulking men. This was not going to end well.

"Good, I like 'em *sssssspicy*," one of them said.

"First of all, you guys need to see a speech therapist. And maybe a dermatologist, too. I can help you find one. I am good at finding things. Just let me grab my phone," she took a step towards her purse, but one of the three blocked her path.

Whoa. She didn't even see him move. Something was not right here. Fergie backed up a step, watching in horror as vertical lids flicked over that assailant's eyes.

Like Jessenia's pet lizard's eyes, she whimpered.

Panic set in. These dudes were so not normal. Fergie dropped her lipstick, ignoring the snickers of another of the trio.

"What the h-hell?" she stuttered.

Okay, Fergie maybe spent a lot of her time daydreaming with her head buried in books or scouring websites for info when she was between jobs. It was one of her vices, or so people said. Personally, she didn't see the problem with being a closet-nerd.

She just loved to read. Still, never in all the time she'd spent looking up facts and studying lore, had she ever thought to come face to face with any of the wacky creatures in her books and websites.

She clenched her jaw, this was real. Her own eyes weren't playing tricks on her. These men were not human.

"Oh, *sssssweeetie*, you'll hurt our feelings," the third one inched closer, "we *jusssst* want a *tasssste*."

"You can just back the hell up!" she held up her hand in a feeble attempt to ward off the brute, "What the hell are you guys?" she asked again.

"You're about to find out," the biggest of the three reached out and grabbed her arm.

He pulled and Fergie, being herself, slid on the slick asphalt. To keep from toppling forward, she had no choice but to grab onto her attacker with her free hand. When she looked down, she saw with growing horror that his skin was covered with green mottled scales and he was oozing some kind of slime. But that wasn't what made her scream, it was the long, gnarly claws that tipped his freakishly, strong hands.

"Ouch," Fergie pulled back from him, shifting her weight too fast in her high heels.

She fell backwards, landing on her ass, which of course, made her scream again. The asphalt was uneven and damn it, it was hard too. It stung even her plump bottom, but that still didn't hurt as much as the three long scratches on her forearm.

"I'm bleeding!" she shrieked once she realized he broke skin.

Red droplets welled up from the laceration and she suddenly felt woozy. She looked up and was confused. The giant reptile-man who'd just attacked her was flying.

Wait, not flying exactly. He was being lifted into the air, and, *ooh*, tossed away like the piece of trash he was! But what if whoever just attacked him was coming after her next? Fergie swallowed down her next scream and found the source of her assailant's sudden airborne abilities.

Holy hotness. She stole a quick glance at the man, all six and a half feet of him, that stood in a defensive position in front of her. The hiss of her remaining attackers had her eyes darting to them, but the resounding snarl coming from her rescuer brought it back to him.

Up and up she looked to search out the source of that ferocious sound. She wanted to see his face, to look into his eyes to determine if he was friend or foe. Fergie had to work to ignore the warm feeling that grew deep in the pit of her stomach as she first took in the pair of large, muddy boots.

Those were followed by big, strong calves, and thick, muscular thighs encased in tight denim. She bit her tongue, glancing over the impossibly large bulge beneath the stranger's fly, and allowed her gaze to travel even further up. She noted with giddy pleasure the rock hard abs, defined pecs, and bulging arms that were outlined to perfection in the thin white cotton t-shirt he wore.

Finally, she got a look at her hero's face. Fergie almost swallowed her tongue as her eyes met the glittering sapphire stare of the hottest guy she'd ever seen. Dark, short-cropped curls crowned his head, complete with a smattering of facial hair that seemed to thicken before her eyes. A trick of the light no doubt, but it was his rough-hewn features that made him all the more mouthwatering.

The stranger seemed to growl at her, but she was positive he wasn't hostile. Somehow, she knew he was there to help. Just like she knew out of all the men there, he was the deadliest.

"Are you okay?" he growled, and she nodded in turn.

Knowing he was on her side made her tingle all over. No, Fergie wasn't scared of him. He was definitely stronger, rougher, and tougher than those other guys, and that knowledge warmed her further still. The stranger nodded once at her, his eyes glowing in the darkness. Nope, frightened was not the word she would use to describe her reaction to the man.

Turned on. Lustful. Okay, plain old *horny* were all better words for what she was feeling. His nostrils flared slightly, and his gaze dropped to her blouse where her hardened nipples were surely visible through the light cream-colored fabric.

Damn girl. This was so not the right time for her headlights to be on and her panties to grow damp. The heated look lasted for only a flash, but in that brief moment he'd managed to take her in from top to bottom in a way that made her want to climb up his mountain of a body and take him for a ride.

Yowza. She had never had such a knee-jerk reaction to a man before. Never felt this kind of sudden and fierce attraction to one. It was like her body recognized him as its master and was demanding some attention.

What the hell was going on? Fergie shook her head and his gaze returned once more to where her wound was now full-on bleeding.

Oh, great. More blood. She felt dizzy as she watched the red liquid pool and drip down to her lap. Her skirt sucked up the droplets, turning the smart khaki into a muddy color in the darkness. Fergie felt nauseous, but before she could give in to that unpleasant sensation, her attention snapped back to him.

Her hero's eyes seemed to glow even brighter than before. A trick of the light, maybe? Then a louder, more menacing snarl ripped from his throat and she gasped in surprise. That sound was not altogether human. She cried out a warning just as the stranger turned lightning quick to meet the oncoming lunge of the remaining two goons.

"Watch out!"

Fergie remained frozen in place on the ground.

She was in shock, she realized. Or at least she was until one of the men landed right next to her and reached for her heel clad foot.

"Oh, no you don't, these are *Christian Louboutin's*," she grumbled and kicked at the man's green tinted hand, "do you have any idea how many days I went without lunch to buy these!"

She kicked at him again but missed as he seemed to float out of reach. Like his buddy before him, green-boy here floated up and tossed away from her before she could connect. Too bad. She really wanted to kick his ass for ruining her outfit.

She didn't have time to reflect on that as two firm hands suddenly wrapped around her arms. Fergie squealed at the sudden appearance of a pony-tail wearing man. He pulled her to the side and squatted down.

"Miss," he nodded his head, "I think we better get you out of here," he picked her up off the ground.

Fergie hardly had time to catch a breath before the large man stood her on her feet and shoved her behind him. He'd moved so fast, she hardly noticed it. Taller than her rescuer, but not as muscular, and not as devastatingly gorgeous in her opinion.

Still, he seemed to be protecting her. He backed up a step, and she did the same, reaching out to hold his arm as her heels slid again on something she'd rather not think about.

Her rescuer had beaten the stuffing out of those three punks. Like literally.

There were copious amounts of blood, not hers, ooze, a few actual teeth, and other crap on the pavement. She backed up another step and squeaked as she slid again. Fergie squeezed pony-tail man's arm tighter.

The other man whom she thought of as her *rescuer* turned around at the sound. Having pummeled the last of the three assailants into dust, he was now free to come over and introduce himself. Or so she hoped.

Fergie wanted to whoop with joy! She was so happy to have gotten out of the whole thing relatively unscathed, and all thanks to him.

Can you say swoon? Fergie waited for him to meet her stare so she could thank him, but his focus seemed to be on where her hand gripped the other man's arm. Letting go as if she'd been burned, she swallowed down the odd sensation of guilt that suddenly filled her.

"Storm, now listen up, *cump*, I just got her out of the way. I didn't do a thing to her," the man who'd picked her up off the ground had both his hands in the air as if in surrender, and she could certainly see why.

Her rescuer had steam coming out of his ears. Okay, not steam, but he seemed to be smoking. Again, literally, and she meant that in its correct sense, not the modern way of misusing and abusing the word.

Actual tendrils of black and gray smoke seemed to surround his body, and that wasn't all. Electric blue lights glowed and circled his hands.

"Um, what's going on?" she swallowed nervously.

"Storm, man, I swear," pony-tail tried again.

All that begging didn't help much. Her rescuer seemed to blink from the place he'd been standing to the space directly in front of her. He growled fiercely and drew back his bloodied fist, socking pony-tail man right in the face, while snarling a word that suspiciously sounded like *mine*.

Dizzy from her ordeal and from having the person she was leaning on so abruptly removed from her grasp, Fergie blinked rapidly as he turned to catch her. He wasn't a lizard, but he was surely something else. Something *other*, she thought definitively.

His eyes glowed like little blue lasers and long

fangs appeared when he opened his mouth. He was a bit furrier than before. His beard appeared thicker, and his once short, curly hair, longer now than it had been when she'd first spied the sexy warrior.

That wasn't right. No, it was more than not right. It was impossible. A wave of dizziness swept over her, more than she should've felt from the minor blood loss. Her rescuer tightened his hold on her arms.

The last few minutes had been the craziest in her entire life. Maybe she needed a moment for her brain to catch up. Fergie held her spinning head with one hand and tried to catch her breath.

"Easy," the stranger's deep whisper sent chills through her body.

He released her slowly and held his hand out, *his claw-tipped hand*, in case she stumbled. Eyes wide, Fergie stared at the sharp looking appendage. The man frowned and closed his fist to hide his nails, but it was too late. She wobbled unsteadily, and he raised his hand once more. This time, she squeaked.

"Sorry about that, it's just my Wolf. He is still agitated," he grumbled the explanation, but all she heard was the word *wolf*.

"I'm sorry, what?" she stopped and looked at him dead on.

"My Wolf," he repeated.

"Ooh-kayy," she knew her eyebrows were somewhere up in her hairline, but what else could she say.

Dizziness hit her again, and she blinked her eyes. Shit. This had never happened to her. Oh hell.

"Um, Mr. Wolf?" she cleared her throat.

"Yes," he said one eyebrow quirked.

"I think, I'm gonna," but that was all she got out before blackness swallowed her.

Well, damn.

Chapter Three

"Damn it, Storm," Kingston Baldric, Dragon Shifter and leader of Storm's unit frowned at him.

The Guardians of Chaos had few rules, but the ones they did have were important. Like the one about no unannounced visitors, especially of the human kind. But what was he to do? Storm held his ground while the Dragon growled from his position in the hallway of the Keep.

He wasn't fool enough to answer the angry Dragon. He simply slipped past his leader with the woman from the lot cradled protectively in his arms. He stalked the hallways to his room. The door opened on its own, and he took that for the Keep's blessing on his decision to aid the female.

He placed her down gently on his bed, already having refused to put her in any guest room. Not even their own medical examination room was good enough for her. She was his to help.

There were currently six Guardians in their unit and of the six, two were crowding his space. Storm was the sole Wolf Shifter. Furio, the Horse Shifter, had his head stuck inside the doorway. Kingston, the Diamond Dragon and their leader was growling and frowning from his stance.

Missing were Byram, the sole Vampire of the unit, Elena, a Panther and the only female, and Egros, a male Witch formerly of the Coven Realta. With Kingston's mate there had been seven, but now that Neela had been stolen from them, their numbers had diminished by one.

The Keep, the name they called their castle, was located deep in the pine barrens of South Jersey. Their only neighbor was a Jersey Devil Shifter and his family, but other than that, they were a good hour from any city or town. The location was good for keeping their work a secret from the humans.

He normally didn't mind the isolation of the Keep, or the way they all intruded on one another's privacy, entering private rooms without knocking and so forth. But now he felt anxious to the point of agitation.

It was the first time he could recall feeling so protective of his privacy. It was obvious why, mating fever was upon him. He just hadn't been prepared for the onslaught to be so great.

Amassed of enchanted stone and steel, the very walls that surrounded him were made of magic. The kind he'd vowed to protect. Almost intuitive, the Keep was the safest place he knew, while providing the utmost comfort for its inhabitants.

It wasn't the *where* that bothered his Wolf at the moment, it was more the *who*. Four males and one female lived there with him. All of them were currently unmated.

Yes, his beast recognized the pain that seemed to emanate from their leader after the loss of his mate and as such he knew Kingston was no threat to his female. But still. There were others. Including that idiot Horse who'd touched her at the lot.

Storm's Wolf would simply not allow anyone near her. He could not let his mate out of his sight. The beast was riding him hard. The animal in him knew who and what she was to him. He demanded she be marked and claimed.

"No. You will not mark her unless we know for certain she is what you say she is, and not unless she agrees to it. That is an order," Kingston practically roared, but Storm's Wolf didn't give a fuck.

Yes, he was projecting again. That kind of telepathic sympathy was useful when their unit was in battle, but that was the second time in as many hours he'd slipped and allowed his thoughts to be known. Mating fever was fucking with his sense of balance.

"She is mine, King," he began.

"You can't start thinking with your dick, Storm, we need you here with us," Kingston returned, "Besides, you don't know if she's *truly* yours."

"Yes, I do. When she was in danger, I was able to use powers I never had. It's the sign of a true mate."

"I saw it too, Kingston," Furio added.

The Stallion Shifter was sporting a black eye and stood as far away from Storm's bedroom door as the hall would allow. Smart man. While Storm wasn't proud of himself for punching him in the face, his animal did find some pleasure in knowing he'd hit the man for touching his woman. Never mind what he did to those asshole reptile Shifters.

"How did clean up go?" he asked his leader.

"Fine. Byram said there wasn't much left of the

two men, but he recognized one as a Loyalist sympa-thizer," Kingston narrowed his gold eyes at him.

"Two, there were three of them," Storm interrupted.

"Yeah, well, you must've missed at least one of their carotid arteries then. And why were you there to begin with?"

"To talk to his fucking informant," Storm growled.

He didn't like the questions. He didn't want them in his room. He just wanted her to wake up.

"Uh, anyway, Byram found my informant in the back seat of a car not too far from the lot," Furio interrupted, "he was missing his head though."

"Shit. So, it was an ambush," Storm concluded.

As a Vampire, Byram would've been able to pick up the blood trail of the Reptilian Shifters and the Goblin informant. The Loyalists had no shame apparently. They would hire anyone. Even a bunch of half-wits who didn't seem to know they should never bring a human into the war between supernat-ural factions. The Dragon Shifter's voice shook him from his reverie, and Storm focused on the golden-eyed man.

"It would seem that way. The woman was working you guessed?"

"Well, I snagged her computer, but she doesn't seem to be a librarian," Furio interjected.

"You stole her things back at the library?" Storm asked.

"Not stole, *borrowed*, so we could learn why those goons wanted her," he insisted.

"It doesn't matter. You have to bring her back," Kingston said.

"No," he snarled, "that fucking Gila Shifter scratched her. She could be infected."

"Well, we won't know that if you don't let Byram near her."

"I could claim her. My bite will remove any toxins," he started.

"I already told you, no," the Dragon snapped at him.

Storm snarled, though he averted his eyes out of respect for their leader. He'd vowed to follow Kingston in all things, but this was not part of his duty to the man or the Guardians.

No one had the right to interfere between mates. Not even him. His Wolf bristled. The beast was not happy with Kingston's declaration. The thought of anyone, especially that bloodsucker Byram going anywhere near his mate, was liable to drive Storm crazy. She was an innocent, and she was his alone to protect.

"Kingston, my Wolf just can't do that, you know what this is like. She is my mate, I can't let anyone else near her. I can't let her go. She is too soft for this cruel world."

"Storm-"

"No. If the Loyalists know about her, if that bastard who got away told them about my reaction to being near her, then her life is in danger."

He could not let her go without knowing she was safe. Maybe not even then. His soft mate had been in the wrong place at the wrong time. Through no fault of her own she'd become the target of his worst enemy.

"The Loyalists have already killed one mate. They can't have another," he gritted his teeth as he spoke.

Kingston might be angry with him, but there was no way in hell he was letting her go. She was far too precious. He wanted this conversation over and the two men gone. He was the only one who could protect her. It was his duty. His privilege even.

Mine, his Wolf pressed him and Storm closed his eyes. He counted to three. He knew that Shifters could be possessive assholes, and something inside of him admitted that he wasn't above that.

"Storm, you need to bring her back. You cannot mate her until you explain things, and then only if she agrees. That's an order."

Chapter Four

Fergie's head was pounding. What the heck happened? She'd been on her way out of that old library after having a super-not-fun time researching old land surveys. It had been late at night. No biggie there. It wasn't like she'd had anywhere else to go.

Just home to Jessenia, her snarky as fuck roommate, and to Jeeves her fluffy, but moody rescue cat. Damn feline was going to be the death of her. Shit. She was late feeding him. He hated that. Usually paid her back with a nice surprise on her pillow.

Sigh. What time was it anyway?

"Owie," she tried to sit up, but it felt like there were a million drums being pounded enthusiastically by a bunch of no talented musicians right inside her head.

Dang. Had she been drinking? She hadn't felt this bad since that time Jessenia had insisted Margarita Mondays were a thing now. Fergie had jumped all over that.

Besides Margaritas were awesome and had minimal calories, unlike her favorite drink. Who knew Pina Coladas were like the whale of all alcoholic beverages in terms of caloric weight gaining potential?

Alas, she'd vowed Margarita Mondays were never to be heard from again after she'd technically lost her job at Shethler Real Estate because of one such Monday evening. That was like four or five jobs ago, but it still stung.

Crawling into work three hours late hadn't gone over well with the slimeball Mr. Shethler or his stupid name. Yep, you guessed it. The gross middle aged man had offered her a way to make up for it, but she resigned with a hard pass.

Water under the bridge, as the saying goes. It was all good. Time had healed those wounds, and she had a new job at L-Corp.

Okay, so back to the *where-exactly-was-she-now*

part of the program. Wherever she was, this bed was super comfortable.

Mmm, she ran her hands over the silky sheets and thick, warm comforter. Definitely not hers. The ratty old blanket she'd had since college now sported several tears from too many washes. Her fingers and toes always got stuck in the darn thing.

She should replace it, but priorities. A girl had to have those. For Fergie, when it came to shoes or blankets, the former won every single time. Hands down. Speaking of her shoes.

"Owie," she moaned again as another wave of pain hit her right between the eyes when she'd tried to sit up too fast.

"Here," a deep voice said from very near, "easy now."

A powerful hand supported her lower back, helping her to sit up as she tried to take in her surroundings. It was dark inside the room. Really dark. But still, there was the odd sensation that she was safe.

Hmm. Maybe her scare-o-meter was broken or something. She was quite certain it should frighten her, waking up in a strange place with a massive headache, and feeling altogether rundown. But nope.

In fact, the big, warm hand on her back was rather soothing through the fabric of her blouse. Fergie blinked slowly and turned to look at her host. Her mouth went dry as she drank him in with her eyes.

Big, dark, glossy curls sat atop his head, cerulean blue eyes watched her from a tanned face framed by thick, inky lashes. She had the feeling she knew him. A spring of recognition bubbled up inside of her, and she found herself smiling like an idiot.

Where had she seen him before? It was there in her foggy brain, but it wasn't clear yet. He didn't smile back, but she got the impression he was pleased by her reaction. His breathing was slow and steady, with deep, careful inhales, follow by slow, deliberate exhales. She'd never found breathing sexy. Until now.

OMG. She was really losing her grip on reality if the way he breathed turned her on. Where had she picked him up anyway?

Then it hit her. Images of the almost too-handsome man with glowing blue eyes fighting a band of lizard men came rushing through her brain as she started to recall what had happened earlier that night.

"I was attacked," her scratchy voice reached her

own ears, and she winced at the pain it caused her to speak.

"Don't worry about that now. Here, drink this. It's water," the owner of the pleasantly rugged voice handed her a cool glass filled with what she assumed was water.

Fergie was too thirsty to question it. Besides, she trusted him for whatever reason. Tipping back the glass, she drank greedily allowing the icy cold water to soothe her rough throat.

She'd finished the entire thing before she realized it. Her cheeks grew warm with embarrassment as she handed him back the now empty container. Fergie always did have a large appetite whether it be for food, drink, books, or what have you.

"Thank you," she said, and cleared her throat, "I don't mean to sound ungrateful, but can I ask you a question?"

"Of course," he nodded.

"Who are you? Where am I? Can I call an Uber from here?"

"That's more than a question."

"Sorry, but I need answers."

"Okay, I understand, but you went a little fast back there. Are you okay?" he seemed hypnotized by her mouth.

Fergie bit her lip nervously before she replied, ignoring his question when she did. The real answer was no. She was not okay. Her eyes darted around the room.

It was big. Like bigger than her first apartment. Neat, but lived in. That was nice. She wasn't much of a neat freak herself. There was a huge entertainment center. A comfy looking couch that she could just imagine being curled up on with a bucket of popcorn and a certain blue-eyed stud.

The curtains were an ugly plaid, but they could be changed. And as for the sports memorabilia that decorated one wall, well, she supposed they could be tidied, but she would leave it. She liked sports herself.

What the fuck, Fergie? You movin' in? She shook her head to stop her dangerously delusional daydreaming. She'd just met the guy. And not under anything even resembling normal circumstances.

"What happened back there?"

The handsome stranger did not smile as he considered his words. She usually appreciated a man who thought before he spoke, but at the moment she just wanted to know if any of what she'd been through was real or if it was some kind of hallucination brought on by toxic fumes from the swamp.

Wishful thinking she supposed. She was far too practical a person for her own good. There was just no way in hell she was going to come to grips with what had happened. Not yet any way.

"Look, let's start with something easy. My name is Hudson Stormwolfe."

"I'm Fergie. Where are we?"

"Hello, Fergie. We are in a house that I share with five others, but this is my room. You're safe here."

"Am I?" she snorted.

"Of course, you are always safe with me," he frowned as if it bothered him that she questioned his sincerity.

Oh well, she didn't have the time or patience to deal with his fragile male ego. Fergie had to get back to her apartment, her roommate, and her cat. It might not be much, but it was her life. She took a fortifying breath and looked down at the bandage on her arm.

Beneath the carefully applied wrappings the scratch she'd received from one of those green-skinned weirdos burned like hell. She bit back a groan and flexed her fingers to test out the tightness of her skin.

Well, that sucked, but a little antibiotic treatment should fix her right up. She tossed the blanket away from her legs more determined than ever to get home via the local urgent care facility as soon as possible.

She might need stitches, she thought with a shudder. Fergie did not do needles, which was why even though she was a fan of body art, she did not have a single tattoo or piercing anywhere on her frame. She compensated for it the best way she knew how, with expensive designer shoes of course.

Why would a woman, especially one her size, want to walk on ridiculously tall, skinny heels? To that annoying question Fergie had one standard answer:

Life's short, bitches, make sure your heels aren't.

Speaking of heels. This was only the second time she'd worn the *Pigalle Follies* from an older, but still classic Christian Louboutin line. She'd discovered the red patent leather babies by chance at a new second-hand shop in Morris County. And they were just her size.

One look down her body had Fergie letting loose a shriek that would have made a banshee proud. Something only she could achieve, according to her late paternal grandmother, Nana McAndrews.

Her Irish side tended to run a bit to the fantastical, whereas her Italian blood had her moods running hotter than all the levels of hell in Dante's

Inferno. That last bit was according to her father and step-monster. She didn't hate her dad's wife. She just didn't like her either.

"What is it? Are you injured?" Mr. Tall and Growly dropped to his knees beside the bed and ran his large hands over *and under* her blouse and torn skirt.

His hands brushed down her legs, removing the cause of her upset, mainly the scuffed beyond repair red heels, and managed to turn her mind to other small bits that needed some attention. She assumed he was checking for breaks and bruises, but Fergie could not stop the direction of her wayward, and entirely lustful, thoughts.

A strange, tingly sensation started in the pit of her stomach as his long, callused fingers continued searching her limbs for injury. Of course, their hurried movement slowed once his eyes met her heavy-lidded gaze. His hands slowed as they reached mid-thigh. That maddening, sizzling touch changed from perfunctory to passionate.

Exciting her as he drew little circles over her suddenly too warm flesh. Fergie bit her lip to stop herself from groaning out loud. When was the last time someone, anyone, had touched her like that?

He dropped his hands as if he'd been burned and

turned around. She watched the muscles in his back ripple as he sucked in great, big gulps of air. Like he'd just run a marathon or something. Fergie was having a hard time herself. She nearly swayed right off the bed. Would have to, had he not turned around, steadying her before she could topple like the mass of boneless woman she currently was.

Holy shit, was that hot. Hudson Stormwolfe, was that his real name, was more man than anyone she'd ever met. She seemed to lose all train of thought at his sudden nearness. Dang. What had she been doing? Oh, right. Her heels.

"Those shoes cost me two weeks salary," she was so busy concentrating on just remembering how to breathe, that she didn't care at all about how shallow she sounded.

"I see, I'm sorry about that," he said and his gravelly voice sent little shocks of awareness right through to her core, "well, besides the shoes, does anything else hurt?"

"My arm is still throbbing."

"It does? I cleaned the wound before I bandaged it. I also applied some healing salve, but you should know, it could still be infected."

"Ugh, I was afraid of that," she frowned down at the bandage.

Crap like that always happened to her. She had the worst immune system. Anytime she caught the slightest little cold it was a month in bed or else she never got better. She couldn't even imagine what this would do to her. She looked up and found herself captivated by his intense stare.

The man had the craziest blue eyes she ever saw, not crazy like mental, just really, really blue. Like little pools of the purest water and boy did she really want to dive right in. She blinked and tried to shake herself from the spell he seemed to weave so effortlessly around her.

"Thank you so much for all your help, but I have to go, I need to stop at urgent care."

"Urgent care?"

"Yeah, you know, one of those budget clinics that've been popping up all over the state."

"Look, if you aren't feeling well, I'd rather you stayed-"

"No, really, I couldn't," she blushed, "it's just a scratch.

A knock at the door brought both their heads up and Fergie was grateful for the respite. Any more meaningful staring and she'd be volunteering to strip her clothes off for the man.

"Come in," bit off Hudson, but she could tell he

was not happy about it. Even odder was the way he covered her back up with the blanket.

Fergie looked up and her mouth dropped open. Was everyone here gorgeous? Hudson snarled and looked from her to the visitor and back again with one eyebrow raised.

"Hello, my name is Byram. I'm a friend of Storm's here," he said to her as he entered the light.

He was tall and lithe with light brown hair combed away from his almost too handsome face. The man was positively pretty she thought a little enviously. He seemed to know that and he smiled a bit sheepishly.

"Byram," Hudson nodded at him expectantly.

"I've come to inspect the wound. If I may?"

Chapter Five

His female was wounded and in a strange place, but she wasn't afraid. That was a good sign, he noted with some pride.

Her brown sugar and almond scent filled his room, and he knew it would leave its mark on his sheets. Might as well get used to this semi state of arousal he grimaced as he tried to sit next to her and found his pants a bit snug.

It was hard enough wanting to lay claim to her with increasing urgency every second they spent together, but now that the Vampire was in his room, he damn near lost control.

Byram was a good man. He was a Guardian before Storm and they'd worked beside one another for nearly a century. But he couldn't help it. He did not want the suave aristocratic bloodsucker near his mate.

Shit. Guilt filled him at the unkind thought. When he took his pledge, Byram vowed he would never drink from an unwilling donor. He got his blood from a bank, actually. Storm knew this, but his Wolf wasn't as politically correct as the man.

"Easy, brother," Byram said in a low voice as he carefully opened his medical bag.

"Will it leave a scar?" Fergie asked interrupting their little convo.

"No," Storm answered her before Byram could.

It was more promise than threat, but Byram still snorted at the implication. Good. Fucker should be aware if he hurt her, Storm would be hurting him.

"My dear, I will be gentle I promise. Let me see your arm, please and thank you," he said.

Storm always wondered at the traces of his British heritage that sometimes lingered in his accent and cadence of speech. He knew it had been hundreds of years since the Vampire had set foot in the place of his birth, but still, he often wondered at it.

"Ouch," Fergie gasped then giggled.

"I haven't removed the bandage yet," Byram said and smirked.

"I know I was just getting ready. Hudson? Will you hold my hand?" she bit her lip, and he moved closer to her.

It was good that she wanted him for comfort. A sign that maybe she was feeling some of the same formidable attraction he was. Mating fever affected humans, he knew, but he'd never seen it or experienced it before.

"Here now, he won't hurt you," Storm took her small hand in his and held it as she'd asked.

Such a platonic touch, and yet he felt it all the way down to his marrow. The healthy bronze glow he'd noted in the dark parking lot was a bit paler now after the incident and her consequential wound. Byram unwrapped the bandage carefully, he had to give him credit.

The scent of antiseptic, blood, and Gila Shifter venom reached his nostrils making his Wolf pace in agitation. Something was wrong. The wound was not healing.

"Is it bad? Do I need stitches?"

"No stitches, but I am afraid it's infected," Byram's steel gaze met Storm's, and he knew immediately there was something wrong.

"You know, maybe you can help me? You see, Hudson here hasn't answered my questions yet, but maybe you can," she narrowed her eyes at the deep gauges on her arm.

"If I can," Byram nodded, ignoring Storm's warning look.

"What were those guys who attacked me? Some kind of role-playing groupies or something. Were they in costume? I mean I know some people have strange fetishes. I once saw a picture of some guy who had these little plates implanted underneath his skin so he could resemble a freaking dragon, you believe that?" she was rambling nervously, but Storm couldn't help but think she was adorable.

"Uh, actually, maybe Storm can better answer your questions when he gets back, I need him to help me get some things from my room to treat this," Byram nodded at him.

"Sure," Storm answered.

He needed to do something to keep his mind off the fact that she was lying in his bed. His eyes glanced down as he pictured the way his hands had roamed over her lush curves just minutes ago.

"Storm?"

"Yes, I will be right there," he said to Byram as the Vampire stood to leave, "You will wait? I can have food brought?" he asked her.

"No, I'm fine," she said a little too brightly.

Storm narrowed his eyes, but he had little choice. She might not know she was his mate, but he did and he had a duty to her. One he relished.

He followed the trail the Vampire left down the hall to his room and Storm entered without knocking.

"Well?"

"Oh, you're welcome, Storm, it is my privilege to help your mate," he snorted as he rummaged through vials in the medicine locker in his room.

"I apologize, Byram, of course I am grateful, but what is wrong?"

"What's wrong is her blood is infected. Something is not right with the Gila Shifter's venom. I don't know how, but it seems to have increased in potency tenfold."

"That's impossible. The mucus those Shifters make should have only a mild effect on even normals," Storm growled.

"Yes, well, this poison is much stronger than anything we have ever seen. I've never come across the likes of it. She will need help fighting otherwise she could lose her arm, and worse than that."

"No, I won't let that happen."

"I understand, Storm, but can I ask why you

haven't just told her what she is to you? Your bite would be of more help than anything I have here."

Storm growled and paced the room. He knew his bite would heal the lovely creature that was his mate, but fucking Kingston and his damn rules. But the Dragon had lived longer than any of them. He had suffered losses none of them had ever known. He was the glue that kept their unit together. Storm owed him obedience.

"I am forbidden to claim her until she knows everything."

"I see," said Byram, "well, Kingston knows best. I have some elixir made from evening primrose and devil's weed which should help slow the venom until you get that all sorted."

"Are you sure it will help?" Storm's worry increased, and he zeroed in on the man.

"You needn't search me for deception, Storm, I would never hurt what is yours," Byram spoke calmly, but Storm could feel his hurt.

Shit. He didn't mean that. Storm knew his words were truth, but he was out of sorts when it came to Fergie. Did having a mate make all men mad? Probably. But it was worth it or so he'd been told.

"She is special, Byram. I can't explain it exactly, but she brings new meaning to me and my Wolf."

"I understand, brother," Byram said, "let's get this to her.

The sounds of feet running and a squealed scream met Storm's ears, and he hurried to open the door.

"What the hell is going on here?" came a roar he knew to be Kingston's followed by a thud.

By the time Storm rounded the bend he saw two things, Furio splayed on the floor with his head in his hands and his little mate wielding the baseball bat he'd had hanging on his wall signed by Don Mattingly in 1985 when he'd received the American League award for MVP. That was a fun year for baseball if he recalled correctly.

Of course, that had nothing to do with why his mate was currently barefooted and swinging said bat against his fellow Guardian's head. Storm grimaced. That was going to leave a mark.

"Oh my God! Why'd you sneak up on me like that?" raged Fergie at the Horse Shifter who seemed dazed.

And no wonder, thought Storm as he took in the lump forming on his forehead. His gaze shifted to his mate's, and he frowned. Her color did not look good.

She swayed a little as she stood one her feet and closed her eyes. Storm ran to her side. He took the bat from her fingers, supporting her frame while she clung to him.

"What happened?"

"Oh, thank God!" she gripped his arm tightly and he could see she was looking a little peaked.

"Byram, can you help Furio?"

"On it," the Vampire said, and sounded as if he was fighting his own laughter as well.

"Come on, sweet," he bent and scooped her in his arms, taking the bat from her hands as he did so.

"Really, I'm too heavy for you to keep picking me up like this," she swallowed after she finished speaking.

Storm frowned. He knew she was feeling dizzy again. The effects of the venom were getting worse. He needed to do something, but first he had to set the record straight.

"You are not too heavy," he stated. In fact, he rather liked the feel of her slight weight in his arms. She was perfect for him. The Fates had designed her so, and he was more than grateful.

"I, uh, think I need to lie down," her mouth was close to his as she spoke.

So close he couldn't resist brushing against her lips with his.

Mine, his Wolf growled.

Chapter Six

Fergie damn near swooned as he brushed a perfectly gentlemanly kiss on her mouth and set her back down on the bed in his room. How did that happen?

His hot blue gaze travelled down her body and she followed, noting with horror her skirt was basically gone. She squeaked and let go of his neck, both hands worked hard to hold the torn sides of the long khaki confection together.

Well, dang. She was down a pair of heels and a skirt. Was someone trying to tell her something about her fashion choices or what? The big man snorted, and she looked up which had him clearing his throat to cover the sound.

Great. The smart maxi-skirt had once had a

small slit that ended with a rather cute red-threaded heart sewn just under her knee, but it was now torn all the way up to her underwear line. Embarrassment rushed through her, heating her cheeks again. She could only imagine what was going through Hudson's brain.

First, she attacked his buddy with a baseball bat, then she was half-naked in his bed. Again. He definitely thought she was nuts, and that wasn't the worst thing he could imagine in her opinion.

OMG. What if he thought she was trying to seduce him? Panicked eyes found his, and she sucked in a breath.

Fat chance of that, Fergie. Look at the man. Hudson Stormwolfe was ridiculously hot, and from the many luxurious items decorating his extra-large bedroom, he was loaded.

Doubly blessed, gorgeous and rich, not to mention one hell of an MMA fighter. The man was unlike anyone she'd ever met. Way out of her league. In fact, Fergie knew he wasn't lacking in the female companionship department. And didn't that just make her sick?

Ugh. She squirmed on the bed. There was just too much of Fergie on display for her own comfort. She was out of sorts and in pain from her ordeal.

Bloody, bruised, and not to mention, horny. It was nuts. She felt an insane amount of attraction for the man and he was little more than a stranger.

Not true, a voice inside her seemed to say. It was the same voice that encouraged her to eat that second helping of dessert on a regular basis or to switch jobs on a whim. She really needed to start ignoring that asshole voice.

"Are you alright?" his deeply masculine voice broke through her rambling thoughts and she exhaled.

"Yep, peachy," she snorted.

Shit. Every time she moved the fabric seemed to get further apart revealing more of her ultra-chubby thighs. She cringed, pushing that negative thought from her mind.

How long had she worked on developing a positive self-image? Too long for her to start that crap now. That was it. She was giving up.

"Excuse me," Fergie let go of the skirt and looked at him hoping he would get the hint and back up so she could stand. No such luck, as it turned out.

"There's no rush for you to leave," Hudson began.

Was it her imagination or did he move closer?

She couldn't stop looking at his face. Strong jawline, straight nose, plump, kissable lips.

Ahem, knock it off, she scolded herself. If she didn't stop it soon, she was going to jump him. But Fergie wasn't sure her fragile mind could take rejection. She was better off playing it safe and leaving before she made an ass of herself.

"I'd like to make sure you're a hundred percent alright first," he continued.

"Your doctor friend said I just needed to heal, and you said it yourself, I'm not bruised anywhere else as far as either of us can see," her response was low and breathy. It didn't sound like her at all.

"Except for your shoes," he replied, and there was that sinfully seductive grin again.

The one that made Fergie want to just sit there and stare at him for the next thousand years or so. When the hell had she ever been so corny about a man? She wondered. Probably never. But Hudson Stormwolfe was unlike any other man she'd ever met. He called to something inside her, not just her body, she realized, but to her heart and soul. Uh oh. She must be delirious.

"I'd like to replace them," he said, "your shoes, that is, since they mean that much to you."

"What? Oh no, I couldn't let you do that," she

cleared her throat and shook her head, "I apologize if I came off as shallow, I just, uh, like shoes," her cheeks were flaming now.

"It's not shallow to like nice things and I could never think badly about you, sweet. Besides, it would be my pleasure."

Somehow, he was even closer to her than before. So much so, she breathed in the faint peppermint fragrance that seemed to cling to him along with another deeper, masculine scent that made her stomach clench.

Whoa. He really was massive. With shoulders easily twice the width of her own, Hudson was powerfully built. Strong, as he'd already demonstrated, and tall. He loomed over her position on his bed and she realized she'd never felt quite so small.

"What are you six-foot three?" she asked.

Her pulse was racing and heart pounded inside her chest. It was crazy. Inappropriate. Definitely the wrong time. And yet Fergie was completely and overwhelmingly attracted to the man.

"Six-foot five," he grunted.

"Whoa. That's big."

Were all her responses going to be so blasé? She shuddered at the thought. She couldn't do this here with him. Flirting was not her strong suit.

She needed a different atmosphere. A change of clothes. A pair of clean, unbroken gorgeousness on her feet to help boost her confidence.

She couldn't even imagine what she looked like. Then again her rescuer, *Hudson Stormwolfe*, she savored his name in her mind, did not seem to care about her current state of dishevelment.

"I got over a foot on you, tidbit," he grinned.

"That's not hard to do," she laughed.

"I like the sound of your laughter. You should do it more."

"Oh, yeah?"

"Yes," was his only reply.

Awareness seemed to kindle between them, fanning the flame to her already heightened state of arousal. His size, his scent, the heat radiating from his impossibly large frame, were attractive to her. Everything about him was.

She breathed in the airy light scent of mint and man, and a soft moan slipped past her lips. What was it about this man that made her want to reach up and run her fingers along the bit of scruff that only made him even more handsome? She was not a particularly forward person when it came to sex. She liked sex. She'd had it before, though for the most part it had been rather unsuccessful. Still, she'd never actually initiated the act before, but for him she seemed to lose all inhibitions.

"This isn't normal for me," she blurted, eyes going wide at her own brashness.

"I know what you mean," he murmured and inched closer.

Fergie's eyes dropped to half-mast. Her nipples pebbled inside the bra making the normally soft fabric feel abrasive to her tender flesh. She couldn't seem to control her body's reactions to his presence.

All her girly bits seemed to be paying very close attention to the man. She knew all the reasons she should get up and leave, but for some reason, she didn't want to.

Fergie trusted him. To take care of her, to treat her well, and keep her safe. It was unexplainable, but she just did. Warning bells sounded in her head, but her heart ignored them. It wasn't every day a man who looked like that came along and made her feel like she was the sexiest thing on the planet.

Not even close, she thought. Really, when was the last time Fergie felt this way? There was only one honest answer, and that was never.

She decided to throw caution to the wind. Chances like this didn't grow on trees. Not in New Jersey at any rate. His big body seemed to give off heat, warming her, tempting her. Yes, she wanted him closer. Wanted his mouth on hers. His skin touching, arming hers. His hands on her body.

Yes, she wanted him. Right then and there.

"Who are you?" she whispered as he leaned down, eyes opened, and brushed his hard lips across her mouth.

"You know who I am, *nushe*," he breathed the strange word into her mouth as he fully claimed her lips this time around.

Fergie didn't have a single defense against him. She craved his kiss more than anything else in the world. The sense of rightness was nearly over-whelming as his tongue entered her mouth and dueled with hers.

Yes, she thought as he pulled moan after moan from her throat. He was one hell of a kisser. Fergie reveled in it. She clung to his shoulders, needing his hard body to steady hers.

A deep, throbbing ache flared to life inside of her, starting between her legs. Fergie whimpered as if he was touching her there. She could almost feel him stroking her swollen flesh with those magnifi-cently long fingers of his.

Thankfully, her skirt was already ripped making it easier to maneuver. She opened her legs wide enough to cradle his hard form as he pushed her down into the mattress and settled over her.

She loved the feeling of his weight pressing down on her. So dominant, so possessively male. A whimper escaped her throat as he held her face and tilted it to the side. Right where he wanted her, he held her still with one hand, and plundered her mouth with his.

He felt so damn good. Fergie moaned and wiggled beneath him. Holy shit. She could've come without him ever doing more than just that. Her brain was screaming at her to slow down, but she didn't want to.

"This is too fast," she managed.

Hell no, she wanted to scream at herself. She didn't want him to stop. On the contrary, she wanted him to keep going. Hudson Stormwolfe might've been a stranger a few hours ago, but she felt closer to him than anyone else in the world.

"But it feels so good, sweet," he growled and nipped her earlobe sending tendrils of desire unfurling through her body, "doesn't it feel good?"

"Yes," she moaned, unable or unwilling to lie, take your pick.

He was so much more handsome than any other man she'd ever seen. Glowing blue eyes, strong features, perfect body. And yet that wasn't all. She seemed to know instinctively that he was good and kind.

And how she wanted him. Hell, Fergie was desperate to have him. She was on fire, burning with need, and he seemed to know it.

Intuitively, he gave her what she wanted. Like he knew how she felt before she did. Anticipating her desires before she even knew what they were, he growled and deepened the kiss. Tracing every dip and mound, every curve with his hands and mouth, Hudson unraveled all her secrets, wrecking her for any other man. She moaned around that clever tongue of his, welcoming his invasion as his hard, muscled body moved against hers in a pantomime of what was to come.

Hopefully, the both of them, she thought wickedly. Hell, she basked in the naughty little image of him entering her with that wonderfully large erection she felt pressing against her. Moisture flooded her panties, and Fergie groaned again.

"Mine," Hudson grunted her new favorite word.

It was so hot and raw. The possessive word was not something she'd ever heard during sex, but she liked it. A lot. He kissed her neck and chin, before reclaiming her mouth as his hands dipped between her legs for a teasing little rub.

He didn't let up, not for a second. He just kept kissing her. Pinning her to the bed with his hard body, stroking her mouth with his insanely adept tongue. Fuck, Fergie meant it when she'd said he was hard.

Every inch of his superb physique was corded with thick ropes of muscle. She ran her hands down his back, tracing the ripples as he moved on top of her. His denim covered cock pressed against her core, teasing her with promises of pleasure to come.

Too many clothes stood between them, too many restraints. No sooner had she had that thought then he'd reared up as if he'd read her mind. He worked her blouse open and removed his t-shirt at the same time so she could look and touch to her heart's content.

"So beautiful, *nushe*," he grunted, freeing one berry-tipped mound from the confines of her ugly, but comfortable support bra, "so sweet."

"Yes," she echoed the sentiment.

Her eyes ate up every tanned inch of his gloriously hot body. Fingers traced his pecs, arms, and abs, so immersed was she that she hardly knew what he was doing until she felt his mouth close over her breast.

Fergie moaned aloud as he suckled the hardened nub. Spikes of pleasure shot through her. They were both panting with desire by the time his head came up. She was truly desperate now. She wanted him to shuck away the rest of their clothing, to bury himself deep within her heat.

"Want you, *nushe*," he growled.

"Yes," she groaned her assent as he released her nipple only to lick the valley between her breasts, upwards to her neck, her chin, and back to her open mouth.

"You taste like marzipan," he whispered kissing her and molding her flesh to his hands.

She'd never had anything like this happen to her. What was this godlike man doing with a chubby ginger like her? He pulled away from her, blue eyes scowling at her.

"You're fucking gorgeous. Every strand of that fiery mane of yours, every curve of this spectacular body is perfect. You were made for me, *nushe*, and this," he cupped her sex, "this is mine. I'm going to take you here with my mouth, my fingers, and my cock. You want that?"

She swallowed hard and nodded her head. Yes, she wanted that. Wanted him. So damn much.

"Gonna make you come so hard you won't remember your name."

"It's Fergie," she whimpered.

She was uncertain whether she'd told him her name before, but if they were going to do this, she wanted to make sure he'd damn well remember it.

"My name is Fergie McAndrews."

"You are mine, sweet Fergie McAndrews," he growled and brought her mouth to his, the hand on her throat tightening ever-so-slightly, "if you want me to stop, tell me now, because once I start, there isn't a thing in heaven or earth that will stop me from claiming you."

Chapter Seven

There. He explained it, Storm thought as he gazed into his mate's gleaming butter-scotch eyes.

She was so fucking beautiful. His mind was a buzzing whirl of activity with ways to please her. Like all the cogs in his clock decided to activate at once, and every single one of them was focused on one thing. *Her*.

Fuck, he was trembling like a green pup. His dick hard as steel, he whined with need as he brushed his cloth-covered hardness against her. The Wolf inside him growled, pressing against his skin. The beast wanted out, to take part in the claiming.

True, Kingston had warned him against doing just that, but Storm knew what he was doing. Fuck it all, he thought, that damned interfering Dragon could not stop him now.

Not when his sweet mate was moaning enticingly against his invading tongue. She was so sinfully sexy, he damn near spilled his seed in his pants. He wasn't going against orders. Not exactly. Kingston said Storm had to explain the situation to his mate before he could claim her.

Well, he just did. Didn't he? All he needed was her answer.

"Well, *nushe*? Will you let me have you?" he asked, a slight tendril of fear that she'd reject him held him still.

"Yes please," she whispered and covered his chin, his neck, and finally, his mouth with whisper light kisses.

That was it. He had her assent. Storm growled and took control of her kiss. He was now a Wolf on a mission. Pressing her down into the bed, he hovered above her luscious form. Then he moved.

Tearing the jeans from his overheated body, he was gratified to see the widening and apparent appreciation in her big brown eyes as she took in his naked form.

He was fascinated by that look. Storm had never seen eyes that particular shade of brown. They were more like molten caramel than chocolate, maybe honey or butterscotch were better descriptions.

Whatever. He was a Wolf not a poet. All he knew was her eyes were incredible. Beautiful and bright, and in the center of each was a ring of amber flame. His *nushe* was fiery inside and out. A spicy little morsel, and his alone.

Storm licked the seam of his lips as he took in her own spectacular form from head to toe. She was a curvy goddess of a woman. The perfect mate and exactly what he'd always wanted. He tugged her bra off, using his razor-sharp claws to cut through the wide straps of the functional underwear.

It was a plain, simple garment, but he found it sexy as hell. Besides, it was the treasures it kept hidden from him that held his true interest. Storm growled softly. He looked his fill before reaching out a hand to touch.

She was pale there and on her soft belly, unlike the lightly tanned skin across her chest and arms. Another slice and away fell her torn skirt leaving her in nothing except a pair of pretty little pink panties. Too bad those had to go too.

His female, his *Fergie*, he thought, testing the sound of her name in his mind, whimpered as he skimmed the sensitive flesh of her stomach with his lips and fingertips. He'd already stroked along her sweet sex, but now he would claim her with his mouth.

Face to face with the tiny swatch of damp cloth that attempted to hide his prize from him, he took a deep breath. The scent of her arousal mixed with the subtle almond sweetness that was all her reached his sensitive nostrils.

His inner Wolf howled and snapped his jaws, demanding the man do something already. He leaned closer and placed his open mouth on her heat, sucking her plump lips through the thin cotton covering.

Mine. The sentiment echoed through him like a trumpet blast. He sucked again. Hard. Fergie bucked her hips and gasped. Her wide eyes met his, and a louder growl reverberated through him. Storm snagged her panties in his fingers and tugged until they snapped.

"Mine," he growled aloud.

His sweet *nushe* nodded her head and Storm's Wolf howled in triumph. Keeping her eyes locked with his, he dipped down to taste her honey sweet nectar straight from the source. Fergie nearly bucked him off of her, that was how strong his little mate truly was, as he lapped at her heat. But Storm held true, swallowing down every drop of her moisture until it ran down his chin.

His sweet Fergie's hands found his hair, but she wasn't tugging him away. Oh no, not his *nushe*. He growled in delight as she shoved him closer, grinding her sex on his face, chasing the satisfaction only he could deliver.

He felt the first ripple of her release and went for broke, knowing he had to strike while she was high on pure pleasure. Storm reared up, gripping his cock at the base, he placed himself at her entrance.

He met her eyes looking for any sign of discomfort or change of heart and thankfully found none. Fuck, she felt good as he pressed inside her slickness. Perfect, he thought and sunk into her velvet heat deeper.

So deep. He stretched her tightness until she fit him like a glove. Out he inched, mourning the temporary loss of her sublime sex, and growling his pleasure when he drove in once again. In and out, he repeated the move. Withdraw, enter with hard, precise flexes of his hips that had them both grunting.

Her orgasm grew and grew, coursing through her until she screamed with it. The spasms caused her channel to squeeze him tightly. It wouldn't be long till he followed her lead into sweet oblivion, but he had to claim her first.

Storm thrust once, twice, three times, until her moans reached a crescendo. Then he struck with his Wolf's fangs. He bit down on that tender place between her neck and shoulder, slicing through her soft skin like butter.

The Wolf inside him howled, demanding blood and he swallowed down her life's fluid greedily, sealing the bond the Fates had begun between them. He sealed the wound with his saliva tossing his head back. Storm's triumphant howl was met with her own scream of completion as another wave of bliss washed over them both.

Exhausted and overwhelmed no doubt, his mate's eyes drifted closed. Finally, the beast within him seemed to cease his snarling and Storm tugged her closer, wrapping her soft form in his arms.

Power pulsed through his body and he felt those same changes that had taken place during the battle earlier that night take shape inside of him. Their *matebond* thrummed in his ears.

He could already feel his Shifter strength working to heal her from her attack. His Wolf's saliva would clean her blood of the venom from that Lizard fuck who dared hurt her. His claiming bite might have other side effects, but it was too early to tell. At the very least she should get some of the benefits of his kind.

She was his now, and that was enough of a benefit for him. He had never felt more whole. A Guardian's true mate was a rare thing, he knew and understood that. Storm thanked the Fates for the gift of her and for the added strength that would help him protect her. What had she called it? Blinking. He smiled at the memory.

His newfound powers would allow him to call upon deeper magic than he ever had before. It was like blinking, he thought, the way he moved during the fight. The black smoke that had whirled around him was as if made from the shadows themselves, and now, he had the ability to move through them or between them as it were.

The other surprise benefit were the whirls of blue energy that he'd always called upon to aid him in shifting between shapes. Only now, that energy was tangible, making his punches and kicks that much more powerful in battle.

Yes, he liked the increase in strength. He would use it to keep his *nushe* safe. Odd how that word flowed so easily when he spoke to her. His grandfather was only a quarter Lenape, but he still had

Native American blood and the term of endearment was perfect for his mate. His beloved *nushe*. The woman who now owned his heart. Storm exhaled.

"Rest now, *nushe*," he said and draped a sheet over them both.

He listened to her steady breathing until he felt himself drifting off beside her. It didn't matter what his leader had said. Fergie was his now.

His to love and his to shield.

Chapter Eight

alk about Déjà vu, she blinked slowly and took in her strange surroundings. Okay, not as strange as the first time around, she snorted then covered her mouth and looked at the huge sleeping male next to her.

OMG. Fergie could not believe what she'd done. Holy shit. She'd had dirty, muff-diving, mind-blowing sex with a complete fucking stranger.

She kept her hands over her mouth and nose to stop from snorting again at her ridiculous thoughts. But yeah, he was literally a *fucking* stranger, cause, *hello*, she so tapped that fine ass of his. Score one for fluffy chicks everywhere! And she'd barely even spoken to the gorgeous hunk of man.

Dang. She shook her head. Bad jokes aside, she

had to get out of there. There was such a thing as wearing out one's welcome.

Besides, Fergie needed to think. Now that the body was finally satisfied, because again let's face it, the second she'd seen the guy her ovaries basically exploded. She was like one huge hormone. And that was putting it mildly.

Yeah, she needed to put together the pieces of what had happened over the last twenty-four hours. Regretfully, she slid out from under her lover's arm careful not to wake him. Good thing he was a heavy sleeper.

He exhaled a deep breath and turned onto his side giving her a splendid view of his nibble-worthy glutes. And, she noted with pleasure, he did not snore.

God he was cute. His thick glossy curls were deliciously mussed, and the hard slash of his mouth was more relaxed in sleep. He looked good enough to eat. Definitely good enough for round two.

No, bad girl! She scolded herself and inched across the floor. Crap. She was buck ass naked and her clothes were torn. She couldn't even look at her heels. What was she going to do?

Good thing the man whose bones she'd oh-so-willingly jumped was a certifiable giant otherwise it might be difficult for her chubby ass to sneak out and commence with her well-deserved walk of shame.

Fergie opened the bottom drawer of a sleek black dresser and peeked inside. Score two for her! She grabbed a pair of clean sweatpants and a matching black hoodie and shrugged into them. Carefully, she snagged her scuffed and broken heels, because maybe there was a shoe repair service that could work miracles somewhere out there. Positive attitude and delightfully sore body intact, she inched out the door.

"Shit," she whispered and leaned against the wall in the hallway.

Where the fuck was she? The hallway looked a little like that dungeon room at that medieval tournament dining place she'd gone to for her twelfth birthday. Stone walls were decorated with rich tapestries and gleaming weapons. The occasional piece of sports memorabilia among them.

Okay, so maybe Hudson was some kind of rich eccentric. Fergie didn't know, and truthfully, she didn't care. She wanted to be gone before tall, dark, and sexy woke up.

Having to witness the moment he realized he'd been high off the adrenaline from the fight, and that was the only reason he'd fallen into bed with a plump little ginger from the other side of the tracks was not on her to-do list.

Fergie tiptoed down the impossibly long hallway. At least there was a long plush runner along the undoubtedly cold stone floors, she nodded as she continued barefoot on her way towards what she could only hope was a kitchen and a telephone. Ooh, and a bathroom.

She should've checked for one of those first, she supposed. Of course, now that she'd thought about it, the need to tinkle was all she could focus on.

Ugh. Pressing her legs tightly together, she hurried down the hall until she came to a right turn which she quickly followed. Finally, she saw a door similar to her, *uh*, to Hudson's room, and she tried the handle.

Unlocked. Thank heavens, she thought as she listened to the satisfying click of the knob before pushing it in.

"Please be a bathroom," she whispered as she looked into the room.

Soft light filled the space from a tall lamp in the far corner. Crap. It was another bedroom. It took a moment for her to adjust to the dimness, and even when she did, Fergie was still unprepared for the shock of what waited inside.

Her eyes widened and she bit back a scream as she took in the huge black panther in the center of the room. Glossy fur, glowing pink eyes, and humongous teeth. The animal's claws clicked on the wood floor as it stepped closer to where she was standing. Her pulse sped up and the big cat turned and hissed at Fergie.

"Oh fuck," she whimpered, and took a step back, but the big kitty didn't like that. Not one bit.

It advanced on Fergie, slinking across the room one step at a time. She kept moving until her back hit the wall and the snarling, growling beast continued to close in on her. It pressed forward until its dripping fangs were the only thing she could see.

"Elena, back off," growled a familiar voice, and Fergie turned to see Hudson standing in the hallway.

She had never been so happy to see anyone in her life. Relief poured through her, but it was short lived as he continued to frown in her direction. The black cat hissed again, and Fergie closed her eyes tight and whimpered.

"Elena, back the fuck off," he said again.

The cat must be his pet or something, she figured, because after hissing once more at Fergie, the creature suddenly bounded off. It went back inside the room from whence it came and slammed the door shut.

Hmm, that was odd. Did panthers close doors?

"You left," he growled, and stalked towards her.

"What the hell was that?" she asked ignoring his statement.

"That was a Panther. You. Left."

"What are you like the Tiger King of New Jersey or something?"

"The *what*?" he cocked his head to the side.

"Ugh, never mind," she walked past him, determined to ignore the pull of his fabulous body clad only in a pair of unbuttoned jeans.

Seriously, if she thought he looked good enough to eat before that was only because she had yet to see him like this. All of her girly bits stood up and screamed for attention the second her eyes landed on him. A fact that scared the shit out of her. She'd never been so out of control of her own body before.

Hell, she hadn't even realized she'd stopped walking until he stood directly behind her. The steel bands that were his arms wrapped around her body and large, warm hands squeezed her tight. She felt his hot breath on the back of her neck to the place where he'd kissed her so roughly the night before. Damn, but she loved every second of it.

When his lips found the spot where she'd undoubtedly sported a hickey, lightning bolts of desire and need spiked through her. She craved him. Wanted his touch like she wanted air to breathe. He was in her blood, channeling a path straight to her sex which throbbed with a longing only he could fulfill.

"Mine," he whispered and kissed that spot again.

Fergie wanted desperately to give in to his caveman-like claim, but this was the twenty-first century. Men didn't simply beat their chests and proclaim a person as their property. Even if the thought of him doing just that made her a sopping wet bundle of needy nerves.

"I need a bathroom, and a phone," she said, ignoring her flights of fancy.

This was just a strangely hot one-night stand. No matter what this man thought right now, it would be over sooner than later anyway.

She was just avoiding the muddy confusion that would inevitably end with her gaining fifteen pounds from all the chocolate ice cream therapy she would no doubt need once he dumped her fluffy ass.

"Of course," he said, and took her hand, tugging her back down the hallway to his bedroom door, which for some reason seemed a much shorter trip on the return.

"Everything you need is waiting for you. I will get us some food, and then we can talk," he walked her inside the bedroom to a gleaming blue door off to the left of the bed.

That was funny. She hadn't noticed it earlier. She nodded her head and smiled her thanks. A shower did sound marvelous.

Inside the enormous bathroom, Fergie gasped at the size of the bathtub. It was like a miniature swimming pool. She opened the drawers of the vanity and found a brand new toothbrush still in the package, her favorite brand of toothpaste and mouthwash next to it.

That was odd, she thought but decided to go with it. Turning the crystal knob of the faucet towards the red tab, she watched a moment as the tub began to fill with warm water. Perfect, she thought and went to use the toilet before washing her hands and brushing her teeth. Afterwards, she climbed into the mini-pool.

"Oh," she sighed and allowed the water, which was at the exact temperature she'd always strived to get somewhere between hot and lobster boil and leaned her head back.

The bandage on her arm had come loose in the water and she unwrapped it hesitating at first. She wasn't good with blood and gore, but this was her body, damn it, and she swallowed down any repulsion she felt.

"Whoa," she murmured and twisted her arm this way and that.

The huge, gaping wound from the night before had receded to two pencil thin marks that looked weeks old. Astonishing. A knock on the door brought her head up, and she panicked for a moment.

"When you're ready, I'll take you to the dining room. Breakfast is being prepared now," he said through the door.

"Okay. I'll be a few minutes," she bit her lip and picked up the soap.

After washing her body and shampooing her hair, Fergie drained the water from the tub and stood up. She twisted a second crystal knob and watched in amazement as some of the stones in the wall pushed forward creating a sort of natural spout from the ceiling.

A second later, clear, warm water poured down on top of her, rinsing the remaining suds clean from her body. She gasped in happy surprise as the stream rained down on her from that stone spout much like a waterfall.

She couldn't call it a shower really, it was much more beautiful and decadent than any showerhead she'd ever seen. Large enough for two, to be sure. She allowed one, *or three*, images of Hudson to enter her mind and bit back a moan as she pictured him in the water with her.

Flashes of last night flittered through her brain and Fergie whimpered. No. She could not go there right now. She shut off the water abruptly, determined to get back on track.

Fergie needed to go home. She had to check in with Jessenia and go to her job. That in mind, she grabbed a fluffy blue towel off of the shelf and patted her body dry, loving the plush feel of the luxuriously thick terrycloth.

After taming her tangled mass of hair into something much more manageable, she grabbed a piece of ribbon and tied it back. Then, she applied some lotion to her skin, which tended to dry out easily, and used the unopened stick of lavender deodorant she found under the sink.

It was really strange that he seemed to have everything she needed. Like the bathroom came equipped with all of her favorite things. All she did was think of them, and when she opened a drawer, they were there. Like magic.

Nah. She shook her head. Her taste was pretty generic when it came to toiletries. Chances were *Mr. Studly* probably ordered the stuff in bulk for his nightly conquests.

Kudos to the big guy, she supposed. He was hot. Hot guys get laid. Period.

There was nothing she could do about the stab of jealousy that went through her at the thought of him with other women.

Forget about that, she told herself firmly. On to the next issue. Clothes, or her lack thereof. She looked around for the sweats she'd borrowed, but they were nowhere to be seen. Exasperated, she exited the bathroom with the towel wrapped firmly around her.

"Hey," Fergie stopped in her tracks as she took in the naked backside of Hudson Stormwolfe bent over while he tugged on a pair of jeans.

He turned around before zipping up, and she got a scandalous view of his short-cropped pubes. Since when did that turn her on? Well, how about, since the owner of said pubes had the most amazingly defined *V* that led straight to them.

Gulp. He grinned at her knowingly, but Fergie

did her best to ignore the sinfully sexy expression. His glossy curls were glistening with damp and she realized he must've also taken a shower. Somewhere else, obviously. He froze her with his glittering sapphire eyes and she held herself still even though he seemed to devour her from head to toe with his gaze. She wished she had something else on besides a towel, or even better, nothing at all.

"Uh, I don't have any clothes," she stated the obvious.

She backed up a step as he stalked across the room towards her, his long legs ate up the space far too quickly for her to have time to do more than simply blink and breathe. Her own stare had been so riveted to his, Fergie hadn't noticed the Neiman Marcus bag in his hand.

"For you," he said and one side of his mouth tilted up in what she suspected was as close to a smile as he was going to give her.

"Thanks," she said and took the bag, "when did you get this?" she gestured to the bag.

Fergie motioned for him to turn around before she rummaged through it. Hudson snorted and grinned but did as she'd indicated. Allowing her some semblance of privacy.

"I ordered them online, and had a friend go by to pick them up," he said.

Fergie gasped as she withdrew a beautiful sheer, navy blue panty and camisole set in her exact size. She removed the tags and slipped them on loving the feel of the incredibly soft fabric. Next was a wrap-around dress in a matching color with tiny little red flowers dancing across the material. It was simply gorgeous.

Even better was a certain box she recognized beneath it. Fergie's heart pounded as she lifted it out of the bag and opened it. Inside were a pair of Louboutin's identical to the ones she'd ruined the night before.

Her mouth went dry. She couldn't take them. Could she? When she looked up it was to find those sapphire eyes glittering in appreciation as they took her in from head to toe.

"Allow me," he said and knelt at her feet placing one hand on his shoulder as he lifted one foot, then the other and slid them into the shoes.

"Perfect," he said.

"They're beautiful," Fergie agreed with pleasure as she slid into the perfectly designed footwear. Only, the man wasn't looking at her feet. He was staring at her.

"Breakfast?" she asked, breaking that stare with the one thing she was sure anyone would believe when they looked at her, that she was hungry of course.

What they wouldn't believe was that Fergie wasn't noshing for food. *Uh uh*. She wanted him.

Something inside of her seemed to light up just being near him, something growly, with a mind and possibly a voice of its own. She knew one thing for sure, when the whispered word entered her head, it hadn't originated with her.

Yes, it came from inside of her, but it was separated too. No matter how much she wanted to agree with the simple monosyllabic declaration and the sentiment that went along with it, whispers of apprehension filled her.

Fergie shook her head and exhaled. But that didn't matter, the voice spoke to her again. Louder.

Mine.

Chapter Nine

Storm led his mate to the kitchen after hearing her simple request for breakfast. What a thoughtless oaf he'd been to forget to feed his precious female! He noted her wary expression and realized he was growling again. Shit. He always seemed to be doing that around her.

"Sorry," he said, "this way."

The corridors of the Keep could go on forever if you didn't have a clear destination in mind. It was designed that way to stop intruders and burglars by keeping them busy for hours, days, or sometimes longer. Enchantments and wards such as those were set up all around the large and ancient castle.

Built on sacred Lenape tribal lands, the added magic of the Shifters, Vampires, Witches, and Fae who'd lived there over the years only served to build up its stores.

"When walking about this place make sure you know exactly where you want to end up or you could be lost," he mumbled to caution her.

"Really? You should maybe think about an intercom system cause, well, it is a really big house, with um, wild animals lurking about."

He grunted. Shit. He'd forgotten about her meeting with Elena in her Panther form. The woman was the only female Guardian in the Keep. She was a good fighter. Tough as nails and loyal too. Of course, he didn't like that she'd scared his mate, but that was his fault not hers.

"So, Hudson," his *nushe* interrupted his train of thought, "are you going to explain what that was back there?" she asked the question he'd been dreading to answer.

He held out a chair for her in the informal dining room. The walls were painted a soft gray with little adornment. It felt wrong to him for the first time ever. Like there should be paintings on the wall and flowers on the enormous granite rectangle that served as the table and was always cold to the touch.

He pushed her chair in gently and started removing the silver covers to the steaming chafing dishes that held just under a dozen varieties of food. He'd always appreciated the Keep's mystical ability to have food ready and waiting for each of its dwellers. The Guardians had become accustomed to having hot meals whenever they wanted. A special gift, one he was even more grateful to have now that he had someone to share it with.

"This looks fantastic," she eyed the dishes of perfectly cooked bacon, scrambled eggs, miniature quiches, toasted slices of Italian bread dripping butter, bite sized fruit Danishes, thinly sliced tomatoes with olive oil drizzled on top, and golden hash browns, "um, before we eat don't you think we should talk?"

"I will tell you everything you want to know, *nushe*, but first let me feed you," he began filling her plate with little bits of delicacies he thought she'd like while she poured them both coffee from the steaming silver service.

Something inside of him was aware of her in a way he'd never noticed any other being before. The way her fiery mane seemed to curl at the ends just around her shoulders had his hands itching to stroke the soft strands. The tiny hum of pleasure when she took her first sip of coffee made his jeans a little bit tighter and his own breathing a bit heavier.

Damn. He had it bad. He shook his head and placed the dish in front of her, noting her surprise. Okay, maybe he went a little overboard, but she was such a tiny little thing. He wanted her safe, healthy, and happy above all else.

Storm sat next to her and accepted the cup she offered, losing himself for a moment in her almost too pretty eyes. He knew he had more explaining to do, but he didn't want to ruin the moment.

"This is a feast. How did you have time to prepare all this and shower?" she asked, but before he could answer they were interrupted.

"Oh ho, this is some fancy spread," Furio trotted into the dining room and Storm cursed under his breath.

"Oh, uh, I apologize about the bat," she whispered embarrassed.

"No worries, I'm good."

"Wow, I thought I gave you a lump?" she stared at the Stallion's head in wonder and Storm cleared his throat.

"Uh, I'm a fast healer," shrugged his friend.

Shit. He might have a bit more explaining to do than he realized. Furio snorted amusedly which only served to annoy Storm's Wolf further. He growled at the Stallion who ignored him and zeroed in on his mate with a wide shit-eating grin.

Oh hell fucking no, Storm growled louder ignoring Fergie's openmouthed stare for the moment.

"So, tell me all about yourself, gorgeous," the Stallion winked at his mate.

He waited for the rage to come, but Storm's Wolf merely chuffed in disgust. The animal within him seemed more at ease now that his luscious mate wore his bite-mark on her neck where all could see.

The permanent symbol that would always remain a part of her smooth skin was not the only sign that she was mated. It was in the scent she bore as well. Something his beast recognized and cherished. A sweet seductive mixture of her natural sugary almond fragrance and his own minty masculine musk.

The result was fucking perfect, in his not-so-humble opinion. Just watching her smile and joke with Furio without wanting to kill the man was a pleasant change. She seemed to be taking everything in stride so far. So much so, it humbled him. She was really a treasure. *His treasure.* Storm was one lucky Wolf.

"Okay, so I remember you from last night," she

quirked her head to the side and Storm's heart damn near tripped in his chest.

"That's right, I was with Storm."

"Why do you all call him that? His name is Hudson-"

"Because he'd bite my head off if I called him that."

"I prefer, Storm, from my friends," he answered.

"Did you want me to call you that?' she asked.

"You can call me anything you like," he said, and it was true.

"Alright then, Hudson," she smiled shyly.

Storm's heart pounded inside his chest. So damn hard it nearly burst through his ribs. No, he didn't mind if she called him by his given name.

"Anyway, how are you feeling?" Furio asked.

"Good, thank you. Actually, the scratch is pretty much all gone," she marveled and held up her wrist.

"I see. It's to be expected after the mate bite," the Stallion picked up a slice of tomato and popped it in his mouth.

"I'm sorry, what?" Fergie asked.

"Uh, Furio," Storm didn't like the stunned look on her face.

He knew it was because he'd failed to really tell her what it all meant. Shit. He'd thought to do that now, over breakfast, without an audience. Motioning with his hand for pony boy to shut the fuck up wasn't working though, and the idiot kept right on.

"Well, the old Wolf got you to mate him right? So, once he bit you, he transferred some of his magic to you. Congrats by the way."

"I'm sorry, say that again," she placed her napkin down and sat back in the chair.

"Furio!"

"No, I want to hear what he has to say," she said sweetly and smiled at the other man, "what's a mate bite?"

"Uh," finally the idiot caught on and closed his mouth.

"We can talk about this," Storm started when her whiskey eyes flashed at him nervously.

"Oh, shit, you didn't tell her she was your mate? You didn't explain about the mate bite and what it meant? What the fuck were you thinking, *cump*?"

"It was a little hard to think at the time," he growled, but Furio just glared back at him.

"Kingston said not to mate her until you explained."

"And I did, I told her she was mine," Storm growled back at the other Guardian.

"Okay, I am just gonna go on my way now. So,

this was fun," she smiled tightly, "but, uh, no worries, boys. You're fine. I'm, uh, just gonna call an Uber," Fergie stood up.

"*Nushe*, please, you have to listen," he tried.

"My name is Fergie, not *nushe*, whatever that means, and you two are crazy, so I'm just going to leave now," she backed away from his touch and that hurt more than he cared to admit, "I will send you money to pay for the new clothes and shoes," she gestured to the new outfit he'd gotten for her.

Fuck.

This was not going how he'd planned. His Wolf started snarling all over again. One thing was certain, he could not let her leave him.

"Dude, you need to stop growling at your mate, you are scaring her," Furio chastised him.

Shit.

He hadn't even realized what he was doing. Looking at her wan face and tense expression and the Horse was right. He was scaring her.

"I wasn't-"

"W-Why do you sound like an animal when you do that?" she kept walking backwards until her back hit the wall.

"That's cause we're Shifters, babe, we have dual natures, sort of like animal spirit guides, but we can wear their fur when called upon," Furio winked.

"What? Shifters? Look, I don't know what you are both into, but I need to go to work."

"*Nushe*, last night was special. You can't just go-"

"Like hell I can't, buddy!" she yelled.

A look he much preferred to the scared uncertain expression she wore moments ago. He could handle her being mad at him, but not scared. Never that.

"What is going on in here?" Kingston stalked inside the dining room and took in the two Shifters and the human woman in one glance.

His golden eyes slammed into Storm and the Wolf felt his Alpha's anger down to his furry tail.

Well, shit. This whole thing truly sucked. Storm had no idea how it had all gone sideways and so fast too.

"Miss? Are you okay?" the leader of their unit raised his hands and addressed Fergie like she was a frightened animal.

"I, I think so, but he's growling like some mad dog, and this one here keeps talking about Shifters, mating, biting, and I just really need to leave."

"Okay, try to calm yourself. If you take a right down this corridor and a left at the end you will arrive at the front door. Wait for me there, and I will take you where you need to go," Kingston stated.

"Alright, but I want my phone," she demanded.

"I will see to that myself," Kingston replied.

"Fergie, please wait," Storm nearly lost control of his Wolf then, the animal pressed against his skin, scratching and snapping his jaws angrily at the thought of the Dragon or anyone taking his mate.

"Stand down, Storm," the Dragon commanded, but the Wolf wouldn't hear of it.

"Oh my God," Fergie covered her mouth with her hand and took off down the hall.

Four hands held him back as he tried to go after her. He couldn't stop the snarls and growls from spilling out of his throat, but he would never hurt her. She had to know that.

"Come on, man," Furio grunted and held on tightly, "you're losing your shit, Storm."

"I told you not to mate her unless you explained it all, Guardian! You disobeyed and now you will reap what you've sewn," the Dragon growled.

"She's mine," Storm insisted, and felt himself lose control of his Shift.

The whine of his Wolf followed by a long, mournful howl fell from his lupine lips. Furio and

Kingston held firm until the latter rose up, allowing some of his Dragon to fill his face.

"You will obey me, Guardian, I am the Alpha here," Kingston stated, "I will take the human home and she will be safe. After I come back, we will discuss your transgressions and find a solution for this mess you've created. Now, you will remain here while I tend to the female," his final words were infused with his Alpha powers, a command Storm could not simply shake off.

He sat on his hind legs and snarled at his leader. Fuck him for vowing to obey the pompous son of a bitch to begin with. He wanted to tear into him, to meet his beast claw to claw, fang to fang, to fight for the honor of escorting his mate home.

"Come on, bro, these are not your real feelings. It's just mating fever," Furio attempted to soothe him, but Storm merely growled at the Horse.

He was burning with the need to chase down his mate, but his Alpha's command was final. He had no choice, but to wait.

"Come on, *cumpy*. You know Kingston will make sure she's safe. You can sit here growling at me or we can come up with a plan for you to woo her later on," Furio tried to reason with him.

Finally, Storm saw the logic in his statements.

He took a deep, calming breath and exchanged fur for skin once more. Walking over to the large buffet against the opposite wall, he opened a drawer for some extra clothing they kept there for random Shifts such as his.

Tugging on the sweats, Storm listened for the sounds of Kingston's tires speeding away. He closed his eyes when he found the bittersweet noise and felt his heart squeeze inside his chest more and more with each foot of space that lapsed between him and his mate.

Nushe, his Wolf cried.

Chapter Ten

"So, you're Hudson's boss?" Fergie tried anything to break the ice between her and the rather formidable looking man who was currently driving her back to her apartment.

"Yes, in a matter of speaking. Did you just call him Hudson?" his lips quirked.

"Yeah, that's his name, right?"

"I suppose it is," the stranger nodded.

The stranger was handsome, she supposed, but not like *him*. Hudson Stormwolfe was in a class all by himself as far as she was concerned. Too bad he was batshit fucking crazy.

She closed her eyes to catch her breath for a moment. There was something really weird about what they'd all been talking about in that dining room. Shifters and mate bites, it was like something out of a fantasy novel.

"So, uh," she began, "I need to pick up my room-mate's truck at the library," she said and rattled off the address.

"Sure," he nodded, "I think we have other things to discuss as well."

"Like what?" she pretended she didn't know what he was talking about. Somehow it seemed easier.

"Like Shifters and the fact that you mated one of my Guardians."

"Okay, just hold on, what the hell are Shifters? And what is that word *mated* supposed to mean? Like sex? Cause I am not discussing that with you," her inner sass demon had just woken up it would seem, but Fergie was on a roll now and she was not going to stop until she had some answers, "and when you say *guardian*, do you mean like your *ward*? Like something out of a Bronte novel?"

The man had the audacity to chuckle. He pulled up at the scene of the crime, where she'd been attacked the night before and Fergie shuddered.

"Is this where it happened?"

"Yes," she said and swallowed down a lump of fear.

It tasted bitter, but for some reason she knew she was safe now. Perhaps it was because of the giant black wolf that was watching her from behind the fence. She didn't think to mention it, merely met the beautiful beast's piercing blue eyes before turning back to the man who'd driven her back to the parking lot where she'd left Jessenia's truck.

It didn't matter. He seemed to already spot the wolf in the marshes, and he was not happy about it. His eyes flashed gold and her inner warning bells went off, but still, she felt the need to speak up for the beautiful animal.

"It's not hurting anyone," she said ready to defend the creature with fur so dark it reminded her of a midnight sky.

"No, he's not hurting anyone, but he's also disobeying a direct order," he grunted.

"Look, what's your name?"

"I am Kingston Baldric. I am one of those Shifters, Furio was talking about. Like Hudson Stormwolfe, or Storm as we call him. He is one of my Guardians, and no, I don't mean in some gothic novel kind of way. In fact, he should have explained all of this to you last night before he bit and mated you," he was talking to her, or so she thought, but for some reason his eyes were glued on the black wolf.

"You all keep talking in riddles. Shifters, bites, mates, marks? What does it all mean?"

"This is going to sound strange, Ms. McAndrews, but since you are already halfway there, I will simply say it. Storm, Furio, Elena, and myself are what the supernatural world calls Shifters. You met Byram too, and he's a Vampire."

"Uh-"

"Shifters are dual-natured beings who share our souls with that of an animal or creature thought to be mythological. Storm is a Wolf Shifter."

"So, he's a Werewolf?"

"Yes," he chuckled, "but not in the way you mean. He shares his soul with a Wolf and he can, therefore, communicate with that part of himself, draw on the power of the beast, and shift into his animal with the help of magic."

"Okay, so Werewolves are real and now magic is real too?" she hedged.

"Yes. Magic is real. So real, in fact that we, those of us who live in the Keep where you spent the night, have all vowed to protect it. We are the Guardians of Chaos, and I am the leader of our unit."

"Of course you are," she muttered and went for the door.

She really needed to get off the crazy-town train.

Like now. Good sex was no excuse for losing her mind.

"Okay, let me try this another way. The men who attacked you," he said stopping her in her tracks, "what did they look like."

"I don't know. They were weirdos. Probably a cult or something."

"Why do you say that?"

"Because they had plastic surgery or makeup to make them look not human. Green skin, weird eyes, fangs, and claws," she shrugged trying to minimize how afraid she'd been.

"They were Shifters, Fergie. Gila Shifters to be exact. Like people, not all Shifters are good," he said apologetically.

"Great. Now, I am supposed to worry about man-animal-monsters getting me?"

"There are female Shifters as well. I believe you walked into Elena's room back at the Keep while she was in her animal form. She is a Black Panther Shifter."

"You mean the big black panther with the pink eyes? Holy shit," she gasped.

"Yes," he nodded.

"Uh, I don't have the keys for the truck. They were in my bag, it got snatched from me last night.

My roommate is going to kill me," she grabbed the door handle anxious to put some distance between herself and the strange man.

"I have them here he said and held out her ruined purse."

"There was more stuff in here. Dammit."

"We can search the ground for it," he suggested and his gold eyes looked kind as he began to help her.

"What about the Wolf?" she asked though she wasn't really afraid of the animal.

In fact, the Wolf seemed the lesser of two evils when faced with Kingston. For some reason, the man gave off a seriously weird vibe. Like he was more than just the six and a half-foot tall massively muscled male in front of her. As if that was not intimidating enough.

"He will not cross the fence. At least, not right now," Kingston said.

Fergie frowned and exited the luxury vehicle with less speed than she'd intended. She walked on her new Louboutin's to where she'd been attacked the night before. For some reason, everything he'd told her seemed to resonate with the truth. But how could she believe such nonsense?

"There's my change purse," she muttered.

Kingston bent to retrieve the small bag from the

ground. It had been tossed aside like so much garbage. A few other items that had spilled from her bag were scattered about, and he retrieved those as well.

Yikes. Having the man handle one of her tampons was just a tad embarrassing, but oh well. The Wolf growled from the opposite side of the fence when Kingston handed her one item after the other, and something warmed inside of her.

"Knock it off," Kingston grunted, but she couldn't imagine why.

She stared at the beautiful animal who seemed exceedingly familiar to her. The dark, glossy fur and bright electric blue eyes reminded her of someone. Her pulse raced as the sound of his growl grew louder, calling to her. Fergie turned slowly to face him.

Oh shit.

"Ms. McAndrews," Kingston addressed her, but she couldn't answer him yet.

It was as if she were frozen to the spot. Her heart pounded and blood thundered in her ears. She tried to swallow, but her throat was dry and she couldn't manage it. The magnificent animal moved closer to the gate, his long tongue licked his muzzle as he watched her like the predator he was.

Fergie closed her eyes and placed her hand over her chest, rubbing the spot where her heart was suddenly beating so rapidly. The Wolf whined and her eyes shot back to his.

She really needed to have her head examined. First, she'd been attacked, then rescued, then she'd jumped into bed with one of the guys who did the rescuing, and now she was talking about the possibility that that guy could turn into a Wolf. This was so not okay.

"There is no need for guilt. The need to connect is extraordinarily strong, oftentimes impossible to ignore between mates. That is why we Shifters call it *mating fever*," Kingston appeared directly in front of her and held out the keys, "here are your keys."

"Thanks, uh, you know I don't normally jump in the sack with someone I just met."

"I see," he smirked, "would you feel better if I told you it was fate?"

"Ha! No, not really."

"I am being serious, Ms. McAndrews," he frowned at her and for some reason Fergie felt like a kid being scolded by her school principal, "Hudson Stormwolfe is your fated mate. It is why you feel so strongly about him, why you *jumped in the sack* with him almost immediately. You could not stop it any more than you could stop the tide changing."

"I don't believe in Fate. Everything I do is by choice."

"Yes, that too. Fate does not take away choices per se."

"Doesn't it? Look, if you're trying to explain why someone like Hudson would fall into bed with someone like me-"

"Not at all. I understand I may have misspoke. Please, suffice it to say that last night you met and were marked by your fated mate. He is a Wolf Shifter and a Guardian of Chaos, which means you can expect some sort of magical boon if you will-"

"I didn't ask for any magical anything-"

"Don't be so quick to refuse what you don't yet understand," he said and his eyes took on a faraway look that made her feel an overwhelming sense of sympathy for the man.

"I have to go to work," she whispered, but it was just an excuse and they both knew it.

"Fate can be a right bastard, Ms. McAndrews, but it is still a force to be reckoned with. You see that Wolf there is not just a wild creature any more than I am just a man standing in front of you. It is Storm, or,

Hudson, as you call him," he gestured to the animal behind the fence.

Fergie's eyes widened. This whole thing was getting weird. It was simply too much for her under-caffeinated brain to comprehend.

"I need to get to work," she repeated shaking her head back and forth, "I'm sorry, if I could have your address so I could re-pay Hudson for the clothes, I would appreciate it," she managed to say without spilling the tears that swam in her eyes.

"Alright. If that is all you can take for now, I do understand. What's your cell phone number? I'll text you with all the information you asked for."

She told it to him and walked to Jessenia's pick-up. Thank goodness her friend ran her cooking vlog from their apartment. She rarely needed the truck for more than grocery shopping and even that she accomplished with delivery these days.

Fergie ignored the Wolf's mournful whine and opened the driver's door. At least the truck wasn't damaged. Thank God for small favors. She stepped inside and started the engine, waving a half-hearted goodbye as she drove past Kingston.

He stood by his car with his hand on the back of the enormous black Wolf who watched her go with sad blue eyes. Both seemed to be waiting for her to leave.

She blinked against the onslaught of tears that had started to run down her face. Fergie was not a crier by nature, but this was really too much. Shifters, mates, magic. Who wouldn't be in tears by now?

Ugh. Fergie had no time for this. She needed to get her head on straight. Her new job at L-Corp was on the line, and she needed the money more than ever.

Repaying the man she'd slept with for the delicious underthings, the dress, and the new shoes was tantamount. She did not want to have any debt looming between them. Not when she was so unsure about what had happened.

Accepting extravagant gifts from virtual strangers was not something she'd ever done before. Okay, so the man was not exactly a stranger. He had seen, kissed, licked, and fucked every inch of her silly. Her body hummed with remembering, but her heart squeezed tight.

It all seemed part of some dream. Like it wasn't real. Only the pleasant ache of her well-satisfied body reminded her it had actually happened. That and the sudden abiding sadness that seemed to well up when she thought of never seeing him again.

She found her cell phone at the bottom of her broken bag and dug it out while she waited for the traffic light to change. Her roommate would certainly be awake by now.

"Fergie! OMG! Where the heck are you? You didn't come home, I was worried sick-"

"Jess, I'm sorry. Look, I had the craziest night."

"Is my truck okay? Are you?"

"Yes, to both, and thanks for giving the truck top billing," she snarked.

"Hey, the last time you borrowed her, she came home with two new dents, fuck you very much."

"Ha, funny. Like you can even tell with this pile of junk," she smiled broadly, tears forgotten as she bantered with her BFF.

"Seriously though, Ferg, you okay?"

"Yeah, uh, can you meet me for lunch?"

"Of course, I'll just meet you. Tell me what time and where."

Fergie closed her eyes and thanked God for her roommate. She really needed a friend right now, and despite her unhealthy attachment to the piece of junk Fergie was currently driving, Jessenia was the absolute best friend she'd ever had.

"I'm going in late, so I'll take lunch at one," she said and gave her the address to her new office building.

Exhausted, confused, and unreasonably heart-achy, Fergie entered the L-Corp offices with a drawn-out sigh a few minutes after she hung up on Jessenia. She went to drop her keys in her purse and moaned in annoyance. Dang it! She'd left the damaged bag along with her cell phone in the truck.

"Just perfect," she sighed.

Oh well. She would have to grab her phone when she went for lunch with Jessenia. No big deal. First, she needed to find out if she still had a job. She smoothed the front of her dress and closed her eyes for a brief second.

Hudson had outdone himself with this number. The man had guessed her exact size in everything, and she had to admit the clothes and shoes felt divine. They bolstered her esteem, but at the same time they reminded her of him.

She definitely needed time to think, but after-wards she really wanted to talk to him. Her stomach clenched, and she frowned. Fergie's biological clock ran on a strict calendar. She was not due to have her period for another couple of weeks. The strange mild cramping passed, but it did leave her a little breathless.

"You got this," she gave herself a little pep talk as she punched in the security code on the pad by the double glass doors she'd been given in order to access the inner offices.

Her new Louboutin's made a light clicking sound as she crossed the tiled floor to where her desk sat. Not that she spent much time there, but she needed to talk to Mr. Offner to tell him what had happened the night before. The company had a strict policy and not only had she missed the drop off with the laptop, but she no longer had the laptop. Shit. She'd forgotten it at Hudson's. She closed her eyes, this was not going to be easy. And she thought explaining her tardiness was rough.

She opened her eyes and looked around the room. That was odd. The lights were off and no one seemed to be inside. She'd been so absorbed in her own thoughts she hadn't realized it at first.

"Hello?" she called out and pressed a hand to her chest.

Her heart was pounding and that strange cramp in her stomach was back. What the fuck? As if she hadn't just been through enough. An attempted mugging and God knows what else, a night of unprecedented explosive sex with a man who made her heart and body simply sing, then finding out said man was actually some kind of fairy tale creature.

She wasn't keeping score or anything, but Fergie definitely thought she was due for a little break. Like maybe a smooth day at work where her boss understood her plight without her having to beg for forgiveness?

"A little late are we, Ms. McAndrews," Mr. Offner startled her as he stepped out of the shadows in the corner of the room where her desk sat.

Fergie yelped in surprise. Yikes. When the hell had she ever made that noise? She inhaled and crinkled her nose immediately against the offensive stench in the room. Was it her boss?

The older man's age spotted skin was a little slimy looking even in the unlit room. From sweat perhaps, she wondered. She recoiled after sniffing again.

Ugh. He did stink. Like unwashed armpit and something else. Something rancid and sweet like this one time when she had been defrosting a steak in the fridge. The piece of meat had slipped between the shelves and she'd forgotten about it until it started to rot and stunk up the whole damn refrigerator.

So gross. She'd had to use baking soda and white

vinegar, the one for cleaning not for salads, to get the stink out. Why would her boss smell like that?

"Oh, you scared me," she plastered a fake smile to her face, "I'm sorry, Mr. Offner, I had car trouble," she lied.

For some reason, she wanted, *nope*, that was too mild a word. It was way more than *want*. Fergie *needed*, to leave. Like now.

Alarm bells went off inside her brain, and she felt herself starting to panic. What was going on here? Another man slid out of the shadows and stopped next to Mr. Offner. Fergie swallowed and moved back a step wincing at the click of her heels in the suddenly too quiet room.

This was so not good. She looked from her boss to the man next to him. It couldn't be, could it? But there was no denying the truth, Fergie recognized the green-tinted skin and angry yellow eyes. Of course, now the man, *er*, Shifter, was sporting a few bruises. Probably got those from Hudson, she thought with mild satisfaction. Funny, she'd never been bloodthirsty, but now she was practically trembling with the need for revenge.

"You," she spat the word.

She forced herself to swallow down a scream, putting her hand over her mouth to stem the sound as the man's skin became a mottled, darker green color before her very eyes.

"Hello again, *sssslut*," his vertical eyelids blinked rapidly over yellow eyes distracting her from his words.

"It seems you have been busy, Ms. McAndrews. A mating mark is quite the prize, is it not? Tell me, where is this Wolf of yours?"

"I don't know what you are talking about," she replied.

"That's a shame really. Good secretaries are so hard to find," Mr. Offner said.

"Hey, I am a research assistant, buddy! And that guy is not normal, in fact, he attacked me last night," she pointed at the lizard-man and took another step back only to bump into something. The wall, perhaps?

Said wall hissed in her ear and this time she did scream. Fergie whirled around. Another green-skinned assailant with scales and a forked tongue closed in on her. He grabbed her face with his claw-tipped hands and she struggled to get away. It was no use. He was too strong.

"*Thissss* one is *ssssweet*," he leaned forward, licking her face.

Fergie grabbed his arm in an effort to move him,

growling in disgust. He simply squeezed her face harder. She was not going down like this. Not without a fight. She let her hand fly and smacked the beast across his scaly face.

"You bitch," he drew his fist back, and she closed her eyes waiting for impact. Thankfully, it never came.

"No more of that," Mr. Offner snapped.

When she opened her eyes, it was to see the Shifter struggling to drop his arm which seemed frozen in place. The good news was he let go of her and she scrambled away from him. Her cheeks hurt, and she rubbed her jaw.

"She is far too valuable a hostage for you to kill with your poisoned tongue or bruise with your fists."

"She hit me," said the man.

"Yes, she did, but it does not matter. We will use her to break the Guardians. We will make them pay," he cackled evilly, but Fergie was having a difficult time following since she was currently seeing spots.

The place on her cheek where the guy had licked her was burning and tingling like when she'd gotten a bite from a jellyfish down the shore last year. Her stomach cramped and chest squeezed.

Shit. Fergie did not want to pass out in front of these three, but she didn't think she had a choice.

The spots swimming in front of her eyes grew darker. She tried to walk, but she couldn't move, her arms and legs felt so very heavy.

She fell to the floor, unable to move any part of her body as Mr. Offner leaned over her with that same evil smile and that horrible stench clinging to him.

"There now Ms. McAndrews, you will be easier to handle like this. Pick her up," he ordered his men.

Fergie tried to scream, but she couldn't make a sound. Panic had her pulse racing, as she struggled to stay awake. She did not want the darkness to take her, didn't want to be at Mr. Offner's mercy. He was dangerous, evil.

Where were they taking her? Would she survive? Questions flooded her brain as she was lifted and thrown over a huge shoulder like a sack of potatoes.

Terror and regret warred with each other and she couldn't wipe the tears that leaked out of her eyes.

Hudson, she screamed inside her mind's eye for him. She wanted Hudson. Why did she leave him like that? Was she so jaded a woman she couldn't admit what she'd felt from the minute she'd seen him in that parking lot.

Who cares if it was crazy or too soon? Fergie was in love with the big sexy man. It was too late now anyway. She was going to die, and he would never know how she felt about him.

Everyone always said stupid shit like how they were going to live each day like it was their last, but how many really did it. No one. Not one person she knew would ever admit so easily how they felt about another.

She couldn't think why. Why was it so important for people to deny their emotions? She didn't want it to end like this. To have it be over before it began. One night wasn't enough. Fergie wanted more. She was greedy, she supposed, but so what?

Hudson, I'm so sorry I didn't give us a chance. I love you, my beautiful Wolf, she thought as the blackness closed in on her.

And then, nothing.

Chapter Eleven

"What the fuck, Storm," Kingston growled at him the second his mate drove away.

Storm whined from his lupine throat and moved to follow her, but that damned Dragon grabbed him by the scruff. He was probably the only man in the world who could get away with such a move, but that was only because the Wolf knew his Alpha.

There was that one little fact. But he also knew that even his Wolf's sharp teeth would barely scratch the Dragon Shifter's tough as nails hide. The fucker.

"That is because I am a Diamond Dragon, fuckwad. Your teeth would break. Now, get in the back," the Dragon commanded and Storm obeyed, albeit reluctantly.

He wouldn't risk changing to his human form in public when anyone could be watching. Especially in this age of smart phone recordings and vloggers posting every dang thing as a supernatural phenomenon.

The world kind of sucked for paranormals these days. But whatever. He didn't care about any of that right then. No, he only wanted his mate.

The need to follow her, to ensure her safety burned within him. But first things first. Storm supposed he'd earned the tongue lashing he was currently receiving from his boss. Kingston stopped in the large circular driveway once they'd made it back to the Keep. He was too damned far away from her, he snarled. He ignored the Dragon's slamming of the car door and shifted back to his skin before exiting. Storm stalked into the house naked, and like most of his kind, he did not give a fuck.

Nudity was commonplace among Shifters since you couldn't keep your clothes on when swapping skins. Of course, it was bad etiquette to stare when someone was naked. No one did. At least, no one who didn't want to get their asses beat.

"Well, what do you have to say for yourself?"

Furio met him at the door and *tsked* the Wolf Shifter as if he were an errant pup.

"Don't fuck with me right now, Furio," he growled and marched to his room to snag some clothes.

"Have all of you forgotten your vows? Everyone to the conference room now," Kingston bellowed from down the hall.

As their leader his word was law. Even the Keep knew that. Any wards or magical sound blockers were immediately disabled whenever Kingston used his Alpha voice.

"What is going on?" yawned Elena as she entered the conference room.

Furio mouthed something to her, but Storm didn't pay attention. Every fiber of his being was on alert. With his mate so far away, their tentative bond was stretched.

Something ached deep within him, like a nervous energy or sense of foreboding. Dammit, why didn't he take her cell number? He kept rubbing his chest with the palm of his hand as if that could stop the pain. But there was only one thing on the planet that could do that.

Fergie, both his Wolf and his heart seemed to cry out for her. One night of having her in his arms had completely changed Storm. He was wrecked, broken, lost without her. Storm was used to being a rough and tough kind of a man. A dominant Wolf Shifter, he was normally fierce and in control. His work as a Guardian had mainly consisted of kicking ass and taking names.

Storm liked his job. He was good at it. But now that he'd met his mate, she was the only thing he wanted. The new power she'd unleashed inside of him pulsed and pressed against his skin. Different from his Wolf, and yet born of the same source, it sought its other half, hungry for her soothing presence.

"Enough!" yelled Kingston.

The entire room stilled. Present were Furio, Elena, Kingston, of course, Storm, and Byram. Egros, their resident Witch, was out on a recon mission. He was a secretive male, but Storm respected the man.

"Ah, so now that Storm is officially mated, might I offer congratulations," Byram crossed his legs and leaned back in his chair in that elegant manner only someone born five-hundred years ago could get away with.

Tall, pale, with a deceptively lithe body type, the Vampire was possibly the strongest being in the room. There was some question on whether or not he could beat the Diamond Dragon in sheer strength, but Storm had his doubts.

He did not answer the Vampire with words, merely nodded his head. There was nothing to be said. Joy was something he should be feeling, but Fergie had left him. He had failed in his duty to explain to her what it meant to be his mate and he'd lost the only woman he would ever care about.

Shame filled him, anger too. At himself of course, for his own rash behavior. He ignored the unladylike snort that came from Elena.

"You should have heeded me," Kingston growled, "now you have marked a human. I had to explain our kind to her where you failed to do so. Do you know how much fun that was? Trying to tell a *normal* what we are and what we do? She is a human woman, Storm. I don't even think she registered a single word of it. She will need time, Storm, and now, because you went off half-cocked, you are compromised and will be useless out in the field."

"Uh, I think it was pretty full-cocked, sir," Furio interrupted, and earned himself a smack to the back of the head from Elena, "What? My room is right next to his," he shrugged.

"Oh, shut up," Elena hissed.

"I can't say I regret it, Kingston. I am sorry I

disobeyed, but this is stronger than your position as my Alpha. The woman is my most cherished fated mate. Even you can't fight the Fates," he stated with more calm than he felt.

"Is it true, about you getting a bonus power? I didn't get to ask you that earlier," Byram inquired.

Storm nodded. The whole room seemed to still. Yes, of course, now he had everyone's attention. Hell, he felt their keen interest down to his bones. Kissing and telling wasn't really his style, but this went beyond that.

They revered fated mates in his world and all too rare an occurrence. He was the only one of them to have found his fated mate while being occupied as a Guardian of Chaos. His position was one of duty and honor. He'd always thought it must be difficult to have a mate while serving the paranormal world in such a capacity, but now that he'd found her he knew she would only make him stronger and better.

Kingston was already mated when he'd joined them, which was why Storm figured the Dragon had never received an additional power boost. Perhaps those were only for Guardians at the time of their service?

"Well? Are you going to tell them?" Furio smirked.

"What? Oh, yes. It was strange because I merely recognized something special about her when suddenly she was in trouble," Storm recalled, "I barely considered that she was my mate, when I felt this strange electrical hum all over my body. When I looked down, I saw swirls of black smoke circling my frame and flashes of blue light around my fists. Then, it was like I was speeding through time and space, blinking, she called it, from one place to the next."

"Walking through shadows," Byram said with awe evident in his slightly accented voice.

"Yes," Storm nodded, "I walked through shadows to get to her."

As he said it, he rubbed his chest harder. Something was wrong. Something beyond his missing his new mate. He frowned.

"Okay, we need to discuss this further. As you know, mated Guardians live here in the Keep, but I did not get the impression Ms. McAndrews would be moving in anytime soon," Kingston began.

"The fuck do you know about it," Storm growled at his leader.

"I was not trying to offend you, Storm," he began but the Wolf in him was seeing red.

Was the Dragon trying to keep his mate from him? Had his leader done something or said something to make her not want him anymore. Irrational, yes, but he couldn't help it. His inner beast was about a half a second away from ripping out of his skin and into his Alpha.

"Storm, look at me."

Storm did as he was asked and looked at the tall Dragon. He was bristling inside. The Wolf didn't care if he was stronger and bigger or the Alpha. If he thought to keep him from his mate, Storm would challenge him.

"All I meant was that she is a human, and this situation will need delicacy," Kingston glowered at the sudden ringing of his cell phone.

Storm was almost grateful for the interruption. A second longer and he'd have been one big, furry, pissed off Wolf. Good thing too. The Keep had a way of getting even with people who did not follow its rules. The old place didn't take too kindly to Shifters suddenly changing in its halls.

Too many ruined furniture pieces and scratched floors to repair, he supposed. Last time he'd shifted during a fight with Furio, the Keep had served him cold tuna salad sandwiches for breakfast, lunch, and dinner every day for a month.

Storm hated tuna salad. Especially with raisins and apples. But, no matter what he'd put on his plate, even if ordered out, that was what he'd wound up eating.

So, yeah, there would be no Wolfing out, he scolded himself. All of the Guardians present in the conference room waited while Kingston answered his cell phone. His surprised expression quickly turned to anger, then something else as he barked off short answers.

"Hello? What? Yes, I know her. Listen to me, you have to get out of there. Leave the garage right now. You could be in danger. No, don't panic. Get to a public place, then text me where you are. My name is Kingston Baldric. Fergie McAndrews is a friend of my associate. We are on our way, and we will explain everything when we get there," he growled.

"What's wrong?" Furio asked.

"It's Fergie," Storm knew instinctively, and panic rose inside of him.

"All of you get in the car. Egros isn't here or we'd use the portal," Kingston growled.

Once outside the Dragon Shifter removed his shoes and clothing, he tossed them at Storm who jumped in the front seat and gripped the dashboard. His Wolf pressed him hard, but the man was positively shocked when he realized just what Kingston had planned.

In a blur of motion, he'd shifted into a two-ton Diamond Dragon with bright, clear scales and glowing gold eyes. He would be able to cloak himself from the humans with his Dragon magic and get them to where they were going in record time.

Whatever was going on, Storm knew instinctively that it involved his mate. His Wolf snarled and snapped his teeth in his mind's eye. The phone inside Kingston's belongings buzzed, and Storm grabbed it.

"Hello," he growled.

"Who is this?" a strange female answered, "Where's the other guy?"

"He's indisposed. You called about Fergie. What's wrong? Where is she?"

"Well, that's just it. I was supposed to meet her for lunch at her new job, but there's no one here. Just her car, well, actually it's my truck. She's been borrowing it. Anyway her cell was inside and this was the last number that texted her, so I took a chance."

"My name is Hudson Stormwolfe, Miss?"

"Jessenia Banks or Jess. I'm Fergie's roommate and I don't know who you are, but I am very worried. Your friend said not to call the cops. I'll give you the benefit of the doubt, but unless I'm not convinced by what you have to say, I will be making that call."

"No! I mean, *please* just wait until we meet in person. The police won't be able to help you."

"Fine, but you have a lot to explain-"

"I know. Can you tell me what she said when you last spoke?"

"She just said something happened last night. She didn't make it home, and that is not typical of her. Fergie didn't sound bad when I spoke to her this morning. Just like she'd been crying a bit-"

"What? She was crying?" his chest tightened.

"Look, I don't know you, but your friend said he could help. I'm waiting at *Corner Coffee* on 4th Street. If you're not here in fifteen minutes, I'm calling the police and going back to the garage."

"We will be there," he growled and clicked end.

What the fuck? He'd made his mate cry. What kind of insensitive asshole did that? Anger and despair waged a war inside of him, and by the time Kingston landed their car in an empty parking lot as close to the coffee shop as he dared, Storm was in one hell of a bad mood. He was a growling, snarling beast.

"Move over," Kingston opened the door and grunted as he shoved on his pants and shirt.

He took the wheel out of Storm's hands and started the car having already heard the address to where Jessenia, Fergie's roommate, was waiting.

When they entered the shop, Storm's eyes zeroed in on the only woman sitting alone at one of the small booths. She had dark hair in a messy bun with an untouched cup of coffee sitting in front of her. Her eyes narrowed at him first, then on every member of his unit, landing a tad bit longer on Furio than any of the others. The Stallion snorted, nostrils flaring as he stared back at her.

Storm shoved ahead of him. He did not have time to deal with whatever show of dominance his buddy was currently engaging in with a human in a crowded coffee shop. Kingston, Byram, and Elena followed him, leaving Furio to bring up the rear.

The five enormous Shifters had to squeeze between chairs to reach the isolated booth. Good thinking on her part. They really did not need to be overheard

"Jessenia Banks? I'm Hudson Stormwolfe, we spoke on the phone," he said, careful to contain his growl, "now, what happened?"

"First off, who the fuck are you people? How do you know Fergie?" she leaned forward and inhaled briefly.

Her dark eyes darted to his face then to the rest of the Guardians with him, lingering only for a moment on Furio. She shook her head and closed her eyes.

"Shit, you guys are all supernaturals. Shifters, right and one Vampire?" she asked.

Two of the men squeezed into the bench with Elena opting to sit next to Jessenia. The Black Panther sniffed and smirked when she turned to meet Kingston's and Storm's stares. They were the only two left standing.

"She's a Witch," Elena said.

"Shh," Jessenia's eyes darted around the small coffee shop, "yes, but I'm more of a kitchen Witch really, and you are all Guardians of Chaos. I can see it in your auras. Now, answer me this, how does a unit in one of the most elite forces in the supernatural world get mixed up with my very human roommate?"

The group of Guardians all looked at one another then back at the tiny, but fierce kitchen Witch. Her magic might be on the smaller side, but there was no doubt she was a devoted friend. Fergie clearly had a special place inside her heart, and that made her important to Storm.

"She is my mate," Storm answered honestly.

It was the least he could do. In that one word, he imbued all the feelings he had for the redheaded mortal who was now forever bound to him by the sacred bite he had given her.

Rumors of Shifters and supes going mad when faced with losing their mates had always troubled the Wolf, but it was one of those things he'd never thought could happen to him. It had been too far removed from his realm of possibilities.

Arrogant. That was the word he'd use to describe his actions or lack thereof when it came to his mate. He'd been a foolish, arrogant ass. Storm had experience with this sort of thing. All of them had. They'd each worried about Kingston after he lost his own mate, but he'd personally had no idea what the Diamond Dragon faced until now.

Just being separated from her was driving him crazy. There was only one possible recourse. He needed to find her, he needed to make sure his fated mate was safe and sound. And he needed to do that now.

"Oh gods! Well, you fucked that up, didn't you?" she slapped the table and rolled her eyes at him.

"I plan on making it up to her," he growled back at the sassy Witch.

"How do I even know she wants you, Fido?"

"Because she let me mark her," he snarled, the woman was too darn snarky for his liking, but he'd put up with that and more to get to his mate, "You tell me, is Fergie the type of woman to fall into bed with just anybody?"

"No way, you jerk! Fergie is not like that."

"Of course she's not! My mate is an honorable woman. She is fucking perfect! Now, please, help me find her."

"Hmm," she seemed to be making up her mind.

It took a moment, but she nodded once, decision made. Storm exhaled heavily. She was going to trust them. Thank fuck.

"Please, what do you know?" he begged.

"Look, she was supposed to meet me for lunch and when I Uber'd to her new job, the office building was empty. Like completely empty. And uh, I sort of smelled Shifters there too."

"What kind?" Storm growled.

"Lizard. Gila to be exact."

Chapter Twelve

Fergie knew something was immediately wrong from the moment she opened her eyes.

What the hell? This was the second time in as many days that she'd woken up in a strange place. Her vision was a little hazy and her stomach hurt like a sonovabitch.

Last time was infinitely better, she reasoned as she tried to sit up and found she could not. Instead of being surrounded by the mouthwatering minty scent that was Hudson Stormwolfe, and his piercing blue eyes gazing hungrily at her, Fergie had been kidnapped.

Bound with handcuffs to a metal cot in some kind of old store room or closet that stunk worse than

Offner. Like mildew and mold, cockroaches and rats. *Ew*.

"Hello!" she screamed and struggled against the metal cuffs that were slicing into her wrists and ankles.

Shit. She looked down and saw her bare feet poking up at the foot of the old metal bedframe. Her new shoes were gone.

"What the fuck?" she grunted.

Was the universe conspiring to take every pair of Louboutin's she owned right off of her body? She huffed out a breath, blowing back a mass of curls that had fallen into her face. She realized quickly that she wasn't able to do much more than a crunch position, and as a certified and proud fluffy woman of the twenty-first century, Fergie so was not the type to do any sort of exercise. Not even by accident. She lay back down immediately.

"Well, damn. This really sucks," she spoke aloud to no one at all.

She relaxed her body once more. Testing her handcuffs again, she grunted as she pulled and pushed only to discover that absolutely nothing had changed.

Fergie was trapped. Snatched up by her putrid smelling *ex*-boss! She didn't really know Mr. Offner well, but he was involved with some bad Lizard hitmen or some shit.

The man was at least eighty-years old. Stooped back, full of wrinkles, he walked with a cane, and slicked the small white tuft of hair that grew on the back of his head down with some kind of old people pomade that made it appear a sickly yellow color.

His hands were covered in age spots and his nails were kinda long for a man. She never noticed his odor before today, but it could've knocked her out on its own, without any help from his minion.

When she'd landed the job, she thought he was simply a figurehead for L-Corp. She had no idea he actually ran things until she was assigned to be his assistant.

It had only been a few weeks, but she'd quickly learned what her boss wanted from her. The man was all about information, and getting his facts in detailed sheets, and the company laptop back in the building before the end of the business day each and every day.

They would wipe her computer and she would pick it up along with whatever she was assigned to research the next day. It wasn't fun or exciting, but that was what Fergie was hired to do. Research and a ton of it.

Land surveys, maps, old newspaper articles and police reports. She'd compiled massive amounts of information, most of it exceedingly obscure. If a report took several days to build, she still had no access to her PC after hours. All the new information would have to be added the next day in its own separate sheet.

Tedious and annoying, but that was how it was done. She'd never missed a single day. Except for last night of course, she thought grimly. Her research at the library had taken a long time, and she'd left her laptop in the lock box in the boot of Jess's pick-up truck.

Hell, if that man wanted her research he only had to ask. Not tie her up for fuck's sake. The sounds of heavy footsteps followed by a slower, more deliberate gait brought her head up. Good, she had a bone to pick with her so-called kidnappers.

The door flew open and the two goons with green-tinted skin entered the musty room where Fergie was currently tied to a stinking dirty, she didn't even want to think about with what, cot. The men looked like they were wearing some sort of make-up or costume, but she knew now what they were. Not human men, no, Shifters, but these weren't like the ones she met with Hudson.

These men had no honor. They'd sold themselves to serve whatever dark plans the crazy old man
she'd worked for had concocted. Fergie had no idea
what Offner wanted from her, but she was going to
find out.

"Hey, frog boy," she taunted one of the men, "so,
you like dressing up in women's clothing?"

"What?" hissed the easily goaded male.

"Where the hell are my new Louboutin's? This is
the second pair you guys have tried to steal from me,"
she taunted.

"Lady, I ain't no frog, and I wear men's clothes,"
the man grunted, and took a step towards her.

"Really? Then what's with the deep V? You
trying to bring back disco too?" she snorted.

"My dear," the impatient sigh of their boss
entering the room had both goons turning around, "I
hired you for your background in research, but that
quick wit of yours would've gotten you the job on its
own," the two men parted to allow him through.

Mr. Offner, still stooped and old as ever, wore a
grotesque smile on his withered face. Fergie had
always tried to think kindly of people because looks
weren't everything, but there was something seriously wrong with this man.

His entire person was just wrong. She saw it

somehow. It shrouded him like a dark cloth, or cloud. Fergie blinked rapidly. Her breathing became shallow, and she felt her stomach cramp.

What was going on? She'd never had such an averse physical reaction before. Her head began to ache. Everything in her wanted to get away from the vile man, but she couldn't move. Stupid handcuffs.

"Well, if I knew you were going to turn out to be a kidnapper and a lunatic, I would have passed on the job offer. Seriously," she struggled to sit up and exhaled in frustration, "would you mind letting me up at least?"

"Not until you tell me where my property is, girl," he sneered.

"Girl? Really? Okay Mr. Politically-Incorrect-Pants, I realize I might have missed protocol with the company laptop, but that was because these goons of yours attacked me in the parking lot of the library before I could bring it to you. Was it my fault there was absolutely no service in that place and their phone lines were down?" she reasoned.

"Why did you not simply give it to them?"

"Because they never asked for it," she retorted.

"Tell me you lot identified yourselves when you approached Ms. McAndrews," he slowly turned towards the two men who went a little bit pale when his attention was focused on them.

Fergie swallowed, their lizard green skin turned the color of faded scrubs after a moment or two. She realized they weren't breathing quite right and her eyes widened.

"Uh, you see, boss," one began to try to explain, but he was barely able to suck in any air.

Fergie had seen enough. Maybe if she distracted Offner long enough help would arrive. Maybe Hudson would find her. Hope sparked inside of her and she wanted so desperately to fan it, but who was she kidding?

No one knew where she was or what was happening to her. No. She didn't want to think about that. The way Fergie saw it, if she was going to die, she was going down swinging.

"No, they didn't tell me who they were. They never asked for my laptop either. What kind of criminal mastermind are you anyway? I mean, you made *me* take a test before you hired me. How on earth did these morons get their jobs?" she growled and rattled the cuffs against the metal frame of the cot she was lying on.

"You know, I think you are right, Ms. McAndrews. Perhaps a late test?" the old man turned slowly, curving one of his gnarled hands in the air and Fergie bit back her gasp.

"Holy shit," she whispered.

It was like when Darth Vader choked the Imperial Admiral in *Empire*. She trembled with revulsion and fear as spittle dripped from the Shifter's mouth. Offner moved his hand once more, the angle bent and unnatural, and the sound of something crunching reached her ears. Fergie closed her eyes as the goon fell to his knees before collapsing in a pile on the floor.

"He's not dead," Offner explained, and wiped his hand on his pants, "yet. Now you," he addressed his other minion, "untie Ms. McAndrews so we may have a civil conversation."

Fergie was too stunned to speak. She felt the cuffs loosen and fall off, allowed that to register before she scrambled off the bed and to the other side of the room aware that Mr. Offner's yellow gaze was following her the whole time.

"I believe you were inquiring about your shoes?"

She nodded. Born with genes that ensured she would remain on the short side, Fergie had always believed a woman was at a disadvantage without proper footwear. It was one of those sayings the women in her family had passed down to her. Well, not her step-monster, but her father's sisters and cousins. The McAndrews' women's unofficial slogan when it came to shoes was sort of go big or go home.

Of course, she'd updated it to reflect her own personality. She remembered the look on Jessenia's face when she'd said it to her a time or ten. Good times. Would there be any more of those left for Fergie?

Life's short, bitches, make sure your heels aren't. Her own words flashed across her mind and she clenched her jaw. Right then, she really wanted her shoes. The floor was cold under her bare feet, and Fergie hated the feeling.

"You will find your Christian Louboutin's under the bed," Mr. Offner leaned on his cane and gestured with his other hand.

"Thank you," she said, shocked he knew the designer's name.

She bent and looked under the bed for her red heels. Closing her eyes, she took a second and pulled them out from under the bed.

"Aren't you going to put them on?"

"My feet are dirty. I'd like to wash them first," she said.

"I see, well that will have to wait, my dear."

She nodded and clutched the shoes to her chest.

Watching him for any sudden movements, Fergie waited for him to continue.

"Ms. McAndrews, where is my laptop?" he asked.

"It's in the boot of the truck I was driving," she answered.

"I can assure you, it is not. You see, Ms. McAndrews we have tracking devices installed on all our equipment. Which is, of course, how we found you at the library after you'd been sent to the courthouse," he closed his hand tightly over his cane and the sound of splintering wood seemed loud in the close quarters.

"What? But that's where I left the computer. In the little lockbox in the back of the pick-up," she said again, aware of a growing unease inside of her.

"And I am telling you, Ms. Mc. Andrews if you insist on playing this game with me you will not recover from what I will do to get the information, do you understand?" he flashed his yellow teeth at her and Fergie's skin crawled.

The old fucker wanted to hurt her. She knew it in her bones. Her eyes darted around the room looking for anything she might use to defend herself, any chance she had to escape, but once more she came up empty.

"Do you want to know why I released you from the cuffs, my dear?" he asked, handing the cane to his remaining minion.

"Why did you?"

"Because you are no threat to me, you insignificant human," he spat the word at her.

Fergie squeaked. She watched in disbelief as the bent and crooked old man began to take off his jacket and shirt. Mr. Offner, her elderly boss flashed his yellow teeth in a parody of a smile that made her want to hurl. His offensive odor grew stronger. The sweet stinking scent of death seemed to cling to him as more of his flesh was revealed to her eyes.

"Oh my God," she whimpered and tried to shut her eyes but she couldn't.

She felt almost compelled to stare as those yellowed teeth cracked under and fell from his bleeding gums under the strength of his own jaw. What the fucking fuck?

"Open your eyes, little human. Did you think I was some weak old man? Come now and see who it is you truly work for," Offner straightened his spine.

He seemed to grow before her eyes, a tall twisted monstrous thing. Fergie's own horror rose inside of her. The sounds of his bones breaking and muscles tearing was loud, too loud. She tried to cover her ears, but something, some unseen force held her still.

Eyes wide, Fergie wanted to scream as the horrible display continued. Tears flowed from too much air hitting her sensitive corneas, but she was unable to blink.

A mash of holes and fangs replaced the teeth in Offner's mouth. When he was finished, he was much bigger and taller than before, though he still had a slightly misshaped hunch even with his newfound veiny musculature. Fergie swallowed down a gasp of fear.

He nodded his head and the invisible force that had held her still dissipated. This monster that stood before her wanted something. Whatever it was, she was not inclined to give it.

"I want the information you researched for me and I want to know who else knows about it," his voice was deeper, more guttural than before. It made shivers race down her spine.

"I told you, as far as I know it's in the laptop in the truck."

"My scouts tell me your truck was compromised last night when those damned Guardians interfered with your retrieval."

"So you did have them attack me?"

"The Gila Shifters are under my employ. They were simply to retrieve my property, but they have failed me. This is what I do to those who have failed me," he reached for the remaining goon, closing his gnarled claw over the Lizard's throat.

Fergie almost felt sorry for him. Almost. Until she remembered he was the one who'd licked her face with his poisoned saliva and rendered her unconscious.

"This is your last chance, now, secure the female, while I ravage her mind," he hissed and thrust the man at Fergie.

The gasping goon grabbed her wrists and pulled her forward to a rusted folding chair that was near to where she'd been standing. She held her heels firmly in her hands like they were some kind of lifeline, then inspiration struck.

"Let me go," she demanded but he simply hissed and shoved her into the chair.

He pushed her down and kept his hands on her shoulders. This was it. Fergie had to try. She grabbed one shoe in each of her hands and held them tightly with the heels facing up. She closed her eyes and said a little prayer to whoever might be listening then she used all her strength and bent her elbows, plunging the sharp stiletto heels into the tops of the Shifter's hands.

His screeching bellow nearly deafened her, but she scrambled out of the chair and ran to the door. Of course, it was locked. She cursed and banged on it, screaming for all she was worth. The sound of clapping from behind her made her turn around.

"Are you finished now," Offner asked with a calm look on his face, "Get up!" he ordered his minion who was currently bleeding from both hands.

"Let us try this again. You, secure her to the chair and you, sit quietly," he waited as the grunting Shifter walked over to her. Fergie met his angry glare and narrowed his eyes.

"*Yessss, ssssir,*" hissed the Gila Shifter.

"The Guardians took you home," Offner said.

He was talking to her again, but she was too busy worrying about what this goon was going to do to her now that she'd hurt him. His bloody hands grabbed at her and shoved her hard into the seat.

"You must be important for them to do that, but I don't have any time to waste,. I must strike before the penumbral eclipse occurs with this next full moon. The darkness will make the magic ripe for the picking."

"What does that have to do with me?"

"You've confirmed the location of the vein of magic I intend to leech from the earth, you stupid filthy human, and now, I will take that information directly from your mind."

"No," she struggled against the Lizard man, but he was too strong for her.

Of course, now he had an ax to grind, and that made him all the more immovable. His claws dug into her shoulders, tearing her pretty new dress. She yelled and struggled, but it was useless. Exhausted and panting, images of Hudson raced through her mind as Fergie tried to wrap her head around what was about to happen to her.

"Don't worry, dear, this will only hurt a lot," Offner's vile grin made her stomach turn as he approached her with gnarled claws outstretched in her direction.

His yellow eyes blazed with power and something that looked a hell of a lot like hatred. Fergie had no idea why the man would hate her, and she did not want to find out.

Offner was muttering something in a language she did not recognize, dark gray tendrils of what she could only assume was magic seemed to spread out, filling the room. The tips of them inched towards her, faster with every word he uttered. The smell of rotting flesh made her gag as it grew more and more with every foul word uttered from his cracked lips.

Panicked, she bucked and pushed against the Lizard man holding her, fighting past the rising bile in her throat, but he was a mountain she could not move. Dammit no. She would not succumb to this. She couldn't.

"Aghhh," Fergie screamed.

It felt as if someone were scraping the inside of her scalp with a hot poker, sifting through her brain, carelessly discarding things he considered useless. Fergie howled in pain. She wouldn't let him invade her mind. But what could she do? She tried. She did. Fergie fought desperately to block him, but she knew she couldn't last forever.

A deep, menacing growl started to build up inside of her. Anger and fury accompanied it, along with real fear and panic. Images of a huge Wolf with blue eyes filled her. The Wolf was angry, and he was desperate to find her.

Hudson. It was Hudson. He was trying to reach her, busting through the smoky ropes of what she somehow knew was dark magic. Her mate was using his blinking power, as she'd called it. He was accessing the shadows and the black spaces between them like secret tunnels to get to her.

I am so sorry, my love, she thought.

Her fierce, handsome Wolf was coming, but he would not be in time. She only hoped he knew it wasn't his fault. Her chest squeezed, and a sob built in her throat. It was too late, but he still fought, valiantly tearing the dark magic binds to shreds.

Fergie wanted to tell him how much she appreciated it and him. She wished he could know just how much she wanted to be with him. To give *them* a chance.

The constant scrapping of her mind eased, and she breathed a bit better now. Hudson had freed her from the incessant pain. The probing of the crazed man she'd thought was her boss stopped, but Fergie could not move.

Sounds of fighting, screams, flesh tearing and bones crunching reached her ears like gory whispers on waves from a faraway shore. That sounded kind of nice, she thought. Fergie embraced the image, she felt as if she was floating.

The whispers grew nearer, but they were still muffled and she couldn't make them out. Her head hurt. She was so very tired. The black Wolf howled long and deep beside her. The sound so pitiful it brought tears to her eyes. She wanted to comfort the beast, but her poor broken mind was worn out, her body too. Fergie was completely exhausted.

Sleep now, float away and sleep, a strange voice whispered in her mind and she nodded.

Yes, sleep sounded good. That deep, black ocean of unconsciousness called to her, and Fergie was powerless to stop the tide from taking her out and swallowing her up. She would miss her friends and the life she could have had.

She would miss Hudson too, her sweet, handsome Wolf who'd shielded her from harm, but now it was time for her to sleep.

Chapter Thirteen

"Did you find her?"

"What do I look like? I'm a Stallion, he's the blood hound," Furio snorted at the dark-haired Jessenia.

Storm closed his eyes and breathed in deep. His supernaturally enhanced canid sense of smell was greater than the other Shifters in the room. He didn't give a rat's ass about the electric current pulsating between the Horse Shifter and the kitchen Witch. They could figure that shit out on their own time. He had a mate to track.

The group of Guardians had left the coffee shop with Jessenia and walked the two streets over to the garage where Fergie had last been known to enter. The pick-up truck was still there, and the engine was warm. That was good. It meant she hadn't been missing for too long.

"She got to work a little late today, and like I told you, she asked me to meet her for lunch. I was early," Jessenia pulled open the unlocked driver's side door, "someone has been in here. She wouldn't have left it unlocked."

Storm growled as he stalked over and sniffed the interior. Gila Shifters had been all over the fucking thing. His Wolf pressed against his skin. The need to run, to hunt down the fuckers who'd been in his mate's vehicle were strong, but first he had to figure out where they'd taken her.

"Storm," called Furio from the bed of the truck, "they busted open the lock box here. Probably looking for the computer I took out of it last night, huh?"

"What? That's what they wanted? Why did you take it in the first place?" Storm barked at the man.

"Hey, don't yell at me. I thought it was strange when she asked me to grab it, but that was the only reason why I did," he hopped down from the bed of the truck, "she told me to before she passed out from that scratch. She looked at me and said, 'I need my purse and my laptop' and then you picked her up. I went and swiped it before we left for the Keep."

"Where is it now?"

"In my room. Sorry, *cump*, I didn't think to bring it," Furio rubbed a hand over his face, a sign he was agitated.

"Okay, so that was her work laptop," Jessenia offered, "this new company was really uptight about security. Fergie told me all about it. Maybe this company isn't what she thinks it is?"

Kingston stepped forward from where he'd been inspecting a drain in the middle of the garage. He seemed extremely interested in what Jessenia had to say.

"This company, what is it called?"

"L-Corp," she responded.

"L-Corp?"

"Loyalists," snarled Storm.

The enemies of everything they stood for. Now it all made sense. The Gila Shifters were mercenaries, guns, or rather, claws for hire. The Loyalists had paid them to hunt down his mate.

"Gila Shifters' are notorious sell swords," grunted Kingston, "you should've seen this."

"What do you want me to say? Want an apology. Fuck, they have my mate!" Storm's Wolf threatened to swallow him whole in a tide of fury and pain. What were they doing to her?

"Storm! You have to get control of your beast," Kingston commanded in his Alpha voice, and for once Storm welcomed his unit leader's authority, "I don't think they've left the building. Come on, focus. I need your nose."

Storm followed Kingston to the drain. He dropped to the ground and breathed. He sifted past the mildew and metallic scents of the actual vent, searching for things he'd find familiar in water drains. Only he was coming up empty.

"It's dry," he muttered and sniffed deeper, "Kingston, this isn't a storm drain. It's an air duct."

"Why would a garage have an air duct on the floor?"

"Makes about as much sense as a drain in this garage," added Furio, "this is an indoor garage and there are gutters outside. Water doesn't get in here."

"You're right. I think there's a room below us and," Kingston pressed his toe against the duct, "this must filter air to it. Can you hear anything? Catch a scent?"

Storm dropped to his knees determined to use his extremely sensitive hearing and olfactory senses to bring his mate home. Worry gnawed at him, but he forced the rising panic to quiet. Even thinking he could fail was unacceptable.

He ripped the grate off the vent and stuck his head as far inside as he could. He took a deep swallow of air and his Wolf tensed. The soft tones of almonds and sugar were there. They were laced with her emotions. Confusion, fear, pain, and sadness being the strongest. All hers. All fading.

Grrr.

"Fuck, she's in there," he took a deep breath, "she's not alone, Kingston. I smell three others. She is suffering, goddammit! The Gila Shifters are there, and someone else. Wait. No! It can't be," he looked up and met Kingston's glowing Dragon eyes.

"Who?"

"Someone we thought was dead," Storm growled, "the Warlock Offner."

He stood up and started searching the walls and the floors. Calling his Wolf, Storm used his enhanced strength to break a hole in the asphalt. Blue orbs of power circled his claws as he ripped apart the ground searching for a way inside. If Warlock Offner was there, Fergie was in serious danger.

"It can't be," Kingston said as he joined Storm.

His golden eyes flashed with fury as his Dragon pushed him. His leader inhaled to try to pick up the scent of their nemesis, but Storm knew he was right.

171

"The Warlock is alive?" Furio joined them with Elena and Byram with him.

"Who is this Offner?" Jessenia asked.

"He's a Warlock, sold his soul to practice dark magic. He is a dangerous man, a Loyalist," snarled Storm.

"He is their leader," growled Kingston, "and he killed my mate."

"Oh gods, I'm so sorry, but what does he want with Fergie? She isn't magic," Jessenia's voice rose an octave with hysteria.

"The Loyalists are trying to gain as much magic as they can to force the supernatural world into doing as they bid," spat Furio, "she must've found something out."

"They want to amass enough power to control the whole of magic," Elena chimed in.

"I've heard of them, but she's a normal," Jessenia looked from one Guardian to the other.

"I don't know, but he hired her for whatever reason and she must have something on that computer he wants. If they find out she's his mate there is no telling what they will do," Kingston stated grimly.

"We need to find a way to follow this drain," Jessenia said, her panic rising as the implications of what her friend was facing became real.

Dread filled Storm. What if he was too late? His heart pounded and his stomach clenched. No. He would not think like that. He stopped in his tracks, opened his arms, and closed his eyes.

Concentrate, he commanded himself. His fists clenched at his sides. He couldn't just bust up the floors with no purpose. Fuck. He had to try to locate their matebond and follow it. It was his only hope.

"What is he doing?"

"I think he is trying to track her."

Storm pushed the whispered words out of his head. He had no room for them. His mission was to find Fergie. She was the only thing that mattered. He exhaled slowly and breathed in once more, allowing the hints of her fragrance to dance across his tongue.

Finally, beneath the haze and fog, separated from the anger and fear, he found it. Softly pulsating, the ethereal link between himself and his mate was there. He saw it, felt it, and he would follow it.

"Storm!"

He heard his leader shout his name, but it didn't matter. Storm allowed the swirling black shadows to swallow him as he held on tight to the thin rope that would lead to his mate. Focusing all his energies, every last fiber of his being on finding her, Storm used his newfound powers to blink out of the garage.

When he opened his eyes a new wave of fury threatened to drown him. His mate was pinned down by a Gila Shifter and Offner was looming over her menacingly. That sonovabitch would die for this.

In an almost berserker-like rage, Storm engaged the Warlock. The bastard was currently attempting to hurt his sweet Fergie using some kind of black magic.

"You bastard," he roared and rammed the misshaped fucker into the wall, enjoying the satisfying crunch of bones when he hit the prick into the cinder block wall.

Next, Storm dug his claws into the sides of the Gila Shifter who still had hands on his mate. The man screamed in pain as he gutted him then turned to face the onslaught of more of them.

Gila Shifters filled the room, and Storm was outnumbered, but he still liked his odds. He placed himself in front of Fergie's limp form. He would be her shield, her protection, until the end if need be. The image of her pale face was burned into his mind.

"Do you still think you can beat us? Didn't your leader already make the mistake of underestimating the Loyalists? I got his mate, and your bitch is dead too! I will win, dog," Offner spat and lifted himself from the floor.

"I hope it was worth whatever you promised the Devil, because I'm about to send you straight back to Hell," snarled Storm.

One arm dangled limply from Offner's side, but he was laughing for some reason. Storm growled as the once normal looking man he'd recognized as the Warlock the Guardians had fought and killed months ago began to grow larger. Offner's cackle deepened, and he addressed Storm in a guttural voice that he hardly understood. He'd been a fanatic before, now he was positively demonic.

"Remove my head or don't it does not matter. You can't kill what is already dead."

"No? Well, I can try!"

"Get him!" Offner screamed, and the other Shifters attacked.

Storm half-shifted, bulking up in size, speed, and strength with blue energy surrounding him, he defended his woman like a knight fought for his lady. He tore through flesh and bone with fang and claw, taking hits left and right.

Finally, he heard the arrival of his fellow Guardians. Good. He was in need of reinforcements. His heart pounded and blood coated his limbs. Some of it was his, most theirs. Fucking Gila monster blood contained venom, but their saliva was what got you.

He'd avoided most of the bites, but it was a close thing. He'd never thought he would be so fucking glad to see the unit of ass kicking Guardians come to his rescue.

Kingston led them all through a hole his Dragon fire had burned right through the ceiling. One by one, his friends dropped down to fight the oncoming wave of Shifters.

Storm barely had time to register Kingston going after Offner which gave him time to tend his mate. The Warlock snarled with their arrival and scrambled with his broken arm in hand to the far wall. Reaching into his pocket, he took out a piece of chalk and started drawing runes on the paint while chanting in what Storm knew was an old dark tongue that had not been spoken centuries.

"Kingston!" he howled at his leader who went after the piece of shit.

The Warlock had truly embraced dark magic. Disguising himself as a Loyalist was genius really, but Storm hardly admired the bastard. He snarled and fended off another Gila's attack. The bastard smelled of Fergie.

"You are going to pay," he promised.

"You know your mate's skin is sweet as her scent, I always did like almonds," the soon to be dead man taunted.

Storm had no time or inclination for suavity. With quick efficient movements he slashed through the Gila's defenses. His Wolf demanded vengeance and Storm was right there with his beast.

With each resounding hit that echoed off the walls of the confined space, Storm's Wolf called for blood. Finally, he used his middle finger and thumb to rip the bastard's throat out. A deep growl filled his chest, but he took no time to glory in his kill. His mate needed him.

"Go to her, we've got this," Furio grunted.

In three moves he ended another of the endless stream of Offner's minions. Storm turned and went to Fergie's slumped form. He grabbed her face in his hands and brought her forehead to his as emotions, he'd never felt before threatened to overwhelm him.

"No, no, no," he muttered, "I won't let you go. Not now. Not when I've just found you. Come back to me, love, come back."

Then he tossed his head back and loosed an ear-piercing howl that had every single being in the vicinity dropping to the ground, even his own team. When he'd finished, the Guardians had rounded up those of their enemies that still breathed.

"Come on, we need to get her back. I know some herbs that will help," Jessenia spoke from his side, and he nodded. He would not give up his hold on her.

"Is she?" Furio clapped him on the shoulder.

"She is alive," he murmured, "barely."

"Then she has a chance," the Horse Shifter said.

"She's got more than that, pony boy, now let's get the hell out of here," Jessenia snapped at him.

"You three go, I will stay with Elena and Byram to clean up the mess," Kingston said, and Storm nodded his thanks.

He was in no state to do more than that. Fergie was in his arms, but she was unwell. He could feel her internal struggle and cursed himself a fool in a million different ways.

Chapter Fourteen

Back at the Keep, Storm settled Fergie back inside their room. He could no longer think of the space as his now that she was in his life. Though truth be told, he'd leave the keep. He'd change his entire life if it meant he'd get to keep her.

Fergie, his heart called out to his mate and Storm dropped to his knees beside the bed. Jessenia had retreated to the kitchen with Furio on her heels. For whatever reason, the Stallion was behaving oddly and crowding the woman.

Storm growled at him. He wanted nothing to interfere with her thought process while she was preparing a healing potion for his mate.

"Will this work?" he sniffed the cup when she'd finally returned an hour later.

Fergie had made no movement or sound in all that time. Her breathing was shallow and her color had all but left her cheeks.

"Storm, why don't you go clean up while we sit with her?" Furio offered.

"No, I appreciate your offer, but I can't leave," he shook his head.

He refused to move from his place at her side, not even to clean the blood and gore from his skin and change his clothes. He simply couldn't. Not until she opened her eyes. Every moment he watched her suffer, every second that passed without her opening her eyes, was pure torture. Seconds felt like days, and minutes were eons.

Please gods, let her wake, he prayed.

"It won't hurt her," Jessenia hedged, "but I can't make any guarantees that it will rouse her either."

"Hey Storm, it's better than doing nothing," Furio said rising to the kitchen Witch's defense.

"Alright, give it to her."

Storm carefully lifted Fergie's head up. His sweet mate resembled a princess out of a fairy tale. The one where the prince had to kiss her to wake her up. If only that would work, he thought, and placed the cup at her lips.

"She can't drink. I'll spill it," his voice cracked.

"Here," Jessenia came forward with a medicine dropper, "let me try with this."

He nodded and stood by anxiously while she ministered to his mate. The woman was a true friend. He could sense her closeness to Fergie through their *matebond*. He was grateful for her help.

"She's my life," he said to the Witch who nodded at him, sympathy shining in her big eyes.

"My mother was mated to an Eagle Shifter after my natural father had died. I know how it is between mates," she said, "there now. She will need rest."

"Thank you," Storm said and resumed his place.

He took Fergie's soft, limp hand in his and brought it to his lips. The throb in his various bruises and cuts were nothing compared to how painful it was for him to see her so pale and weak.

She was always so full of fire. Beautiful and brave, sensual and earthy, she was everything he'd always wanted in a mate. His perfect match in every way.

This was not fair. He couldn't have found her after all these years to have her ripped away by that fucking fanatical asshole of a Warlock bastard. And the fact he'd gotten away made him all the more angry.

Storm promised he'd hunt down Offner after she was better. He would rip the fucker to shreds. Make him pay for even thinking about touching her.

"I get first dibs," the softly spoken whisper brought his startled head up.

Eyes the color of whiskey met his, and he watched in disbelief as they warmed to molten butterscotch. Fergie furrowed her eyebrows and reached to touch his face.

"You're bruised," she said.

"You're awake," he countered and this time he let the tears flow, "thank the gods."

Storm dropped his head onto her belly and kissed her over the sheet that covered her body, holding her as tightly as he dared. When her arms came around him, he exhaled a great deep breath of relief. She was awake now. She was better, and that was all that mattered.

He dropped more kisses on her stomach over the bedspread, moving upwards to her chest, her neck, her chin, her cheeks, her mouth, every place he could reach, whispering senseless words of love and promises.

Nonsensical phrases and touches that she met and echoed in response. He could hardly believe it, but he was so grateful, he didn't dare question.

"I'm so sorry, love, my love, my mate," he said.

"Don't be. I should have asked more questions instead of running. I was scared," she said, and he saw tears trickle down her cheeks.

The pain they caused him nearly undid him. He took her face in his hands and dropped his forehead to hers. Breathing in her scent he willed himself to calm.

"I am so sorry you were scared. Where did he hurt you?"

"No, that's not what I meant. I mean, yeah, we can talk about that later, but I need to tell you that I am sorry I ran from you. I was scared of what I was feeling."

"What do you mean?"

"I mean, I thought I would sound crazy or desperate or both if I told you that, well, I think I love you," her watery-eyed smile reached him and he held her tighter.

"You do?" his eyes widened and pride filled him as she nodded.

"I love you so much, mate," he growled and claimed her mouth in as gentle a kiss as he could muster before forcing himself to release her.

"Why didn't you say that before? I would've

never walked out this morning," she smacked him, then hugged him tighter.

"I was an idiot," he apologized, "but I will never keep anything from you again."

"Good," she said and sat up, "will you do something for me?"

"Anything," he vowed and helped her to stand.

"I want a bath," she said and her eyes glittered at him in the dim room.

Storm steadied her with a hand on her elbow when she would have wobbled. His breath hitched and cock hardened with her presence. Fuck, he was an animal, but it couldn't be helped. He would always want her. That didn't mean he would do anything about it. She needed to get well first.

"Okay," he nodded.

"With you. I want to take a bath with you," she whispered, and he watched in awe as heat filled her gaze.

"Are you certain you are strong enough?"

"Hudson, that man tried to rape my mind. Evil tendrils of whatever filth he's filled himself with scratched at the inside of my head, and I need to chase the remnants away. I need to remember that I am alive, help me," she covered his mouth with her hand when he snarled in response to her frank statement, "No more anger. I need you to help me feel good. I want to connect with you. Please," she begged.

How could he ever say no? Simple. He couldn't. He would always give her what she needed.

"Mate," he growled the word, "whatever you need, I will provide," he lifted her off her feet.

"Shit," she frowned, and he stopped in his tracks.

"Are you hurting? Do you need a doctor?"

"No, dammit," she growled, and he followed her gaze to her feet, "I lost another pair of shoes! I stabbed that green freak with the heels," she snarled.

Relief flowed through Storm and he laughed aloud. He walked to the adjoining bathroom and cradled his sweet, sexy, shoe-loving mate in his arms.

"My love, I will buy you a truckload of them if it makes you happy."

"A truckload, huh?"

"Yes," he sat her on his knee, and turned on the water watching it cascade like a waterfall into the tub.

"I'll hold you to that," she unbuttoned the dress and slipped it off her shoulders, and he helped her into the tub while removing his clothes.

"Let's rinse off this muck before we plug the drain," she said.

Storm removed his soiled clothes and joined her. Fergie reached for him and he allowed her to wash his frame with her tender, loving hands while he did the same to her.

Together they bathed and rinsed, then he did as she'd suggested. Storm plugged the drain and filled the tub with steaming water. He added a scoop of unscented healing salts and sat with his legs on either side of her supple form, loving the feel of her lush shape cradled in his embrace.

"Feel good?" he asked.

"Yes," she sighed and relaxed, allowing her weight to press against him.

"Good," he kissed her shoulder.

"Hudson?"

"Most people call me Storm," he said.

"That's why I call you Hudson," she bit her lip and they both smiled.

"Anything you want, love."

"Okay, I want answers."

"Shoot."

"How does this work? Us being mates, I mean," she frowned.

"Well, I've never been mated before," he began, and his heart swelled with love for her, "but I think we can figure this out together."

"Yeah?" she teased and splashed him.

"Yes," he said, letting the truth in his eyes speak for itself.

Storm tugged on a lock of her hair bringing her closer until their faces were perfectly aligned, then he mashed his mouth to hers. Softly, slowly, he poured all of his love for her into his kiss. Again and again his lips met hers, tongues tangled and breath mingled until they were both trembling with desire.

"Need you, mate," he whispered, teasing her tongue into following his as he traced the seam of her plump lips.

"I want you to need me, Hudson. I've never felt so safe and loved in all my life," her eyes darted to his, and he felt as if he'd been struck by lightning.

His pulse raced as Fergie turned in the water and straddled his legs. Her skin was slick and hot as it rubbed against his.

"Good cause I do need and want you. I always will and I vow to always keep you safe as well, love you, mate," he growled and skimmed his hands up her arms to her vulnerable throat.

Storm caressed her skin, nibbling on her mouth while she rolled her hips, stroking his sex with her own. The heat of the water was nothing compared to the blood boiling in his veins. She was a siren, a goddess, and all his. His Wolf growled, and the man wanted to beat his chest in triumph.

"Now, Hudson, want you now," she moaned into his mouth.

"Anything for you, mate," he promised.

"Hudson," she moaned his name and Storm's entire body trembled.

His cock twitched and his brain short-circuited. All he wanted was to bury himself deep inside of her welcoming heat, to lose himself in the pleasure only she could give him.

After almost losing her, it was heaven to be able to hold her, kiss her, love her like this again. He'd been scared that he would never relish her in his arms again.

"You'll always have me, Hudson, if you want me," she read his thoughts and he welcomed the exchange. Mated couples could sometimes communicate tele-pathically and he couldn't help but think that would come in handy as she positioned herself over his hard length. She held his gaze, waiting for his response and Storm tightened his hold on her bountiful hips.

"I will always want you," he grunted and entered her slick heat with one strong flex of his hips, "mate."

Pure pleasure, the kind he only ever tasted with

her, touched every cell of Storm's being. He knocked the drain from its hold, needing less water so he could control their movements better. Fergie clutched his shoulders, their slick skin made it hard to find purchase, but they made it work.

Storm intensified his thrusts, following every twitch and moan his mate made like a roadmap to ecstasy. Both hers and his. She was breathtaking like this. Eyes lust-glazed, cheeks pink, hair a wild mane of fire.

Yes, Storm thought, she was normally gorgeous, but in the throes of passion she was a goddess. His goddess. He was hardly able to keep himself from spilling his seed like a green pup, but even he had the presence of mind to make sure his mate was satisfied before he followed suit.

Her walls clenched around his length, stroking him deftly with every swivel and grind of her sexy as fuck body. Storm's balls drew tight against his body, ready to spill his seed deep into her healthy womb. But not yet.

First, he would make her see stars, then he'd follow her into oblivion. Grind, swivel, thrust, and repeat. Water splashed around them, the sounds of their passion echoed off the tiled walls. Fergie's moans grew louder, more erratic as he added power and speed to his thrust.

"Do you like that, mate?" he grunted, and she nodded, unable to speak.

Good, he wanted her speechless. Loved her desperate and panting. Fuck yeah, he gave her more. He drove deeper and deeper into her tight sheath. Every move, every whimper, every scrape of her nails on his shoulders, every shudder and moan was his. Only his. He wanted them all. He'd always been a greedy fuck.

"Come for me, love," he growled.

Large hands gripped her hips, he lifted his mate and brought her down hard on his cock. Again, this time faster. And again.

Storm worked her into a frenzy of passion and movement. He thanked fuck for his Wolf's speed and strength in this. Pleasuring his mate would always be a priority for man and beast.

"Hudson, gonna-" she slapped her hands against his arms.

Her mouth fell open in a silent scream, Fergie arched her back. Storm felt his fangs extend, and he leaned forward and pierced the flesh just above her perfect breasts, marking her again and claiming her once more as his own.

The tangy sweetness of her life's source rushed down his throat and her sex squeezed him. His eyes widened as a sharp burning pain seized his shoulder. It was soon replaced with pleasure so sweet, he could hardly breath. Fergie rolled her hips dragging a deep moan from them both and lapped at his skin.

Blinding white lights filled his vision and Storm dropped his head back and howled. Sinking into her was as close to heaven as his Wolf's soul had ever been. Pure bliss, he thought as he filled her with his seed, changing her scent, and mixing their essences for all time.

"Mine," the word reverberated in the bathroom, only it wasn't his voice. It was hers.

Satisfaction warred with pure wonder. Both emotions raced for dominance as he opened his eyes to look upon his glorious mate. Fergie's blood tinted lips were opened and her fangs peeked through. She was breathing heavily, her butterscotch colored eyes glowing as she viewed him.

"Mine," she said again, and he hardened once more inside of her.

This time, he would love her slowly and properly. And in bed.

Chapter Fifteen

"**S**o, what you're telling me," she said between bites of a very large, very rare ribeye steak.

It was so large she'd needed a second dish for sides, which resembled most of the Shifters' places for those of them gathered around the long table in the dining room of the castle, also known as the Keep. Except for Furio. The Horse Shifter was a vegetarian and was currently munching on an enormous cauliflower seasoned with garlic, olive oil, and sea salt. She recognized it as a specialty of Jessenia's.

Hmm. That was weird. She was certain her BFF hated the man. Besides the magic kitchen did all the cooking.

"What were you saying?" Hudson asked, and she resumed her train of thought.

"Oh, uh, so you guys are telling me I'm a Shifter now?"

"Yes," said Kingston, their leader, "sort of."

"What do you mean sort of?" snorted Jessenia.

Fergie growled at her so-called BFF. Turned out, she had quite the secret too. Jessenia Banks was a Witch. And not just because she ate the last strawberry Poptart or finished the coffee.

Hmm. She was a rather ballsy Witch too. Seeing as how she just turned and blew a raspberry at her newly growly and furry former roommate.

"Shifters aren't made with bites. We are not actually Werewolves or what have you. Not the way the humans tell in their legends and myth. However, it is written that true mates can sometimes awaken their significant other's *anima animalis* or animal soul," the Dragon Shifter said.

Fergie frowned at the hard-looking man. His meat was burnt to a crisp. She couldn't really be expected to trust someone who preferred to char their meat black, could she? The fluffy ginger colored Wolf inside of her shook her head. Seemed she didn't like that either.

"You okay, love?" Hudson, or Storm as he preferred his friends to call him, asked.

Fergie supposed that in company she could think

of him by his nickname. She nodded at him. Her lover, her mate, her Wolf who'd shielded her with his very body when she'd been under attack.

Good mate, her Wolf pushed the thought at her, and she hummed in agreement.

"Okay, so I'm a Wolf Shifter now and you are all members of an elite group of supernaturals called Guardians of Chaos?"

"Yes. Our job is to preserve the natural free state of all magic for the betterment of supernatural peoples," Kingston explained.

"Yes, but *nushe*, if you want me to give up my vows," Storm began and everyone at the table stilled.

"Are you kidding? This is totally kickass," she said, and she meant it, "And just think, being mated to me means you get to keep your new *blinky* superpowers-"

"Fergie," Storm looked pained at her description of his new enhancements.

"Well, love, you blink in and out of the shadows and when you throw punches your hands glow blue with your Wolf's added energy," she shrugged.

"I like it," Furio grinned, "we can call you *blinky* now!"

Storm growled at the Horse Shifter and tossed a

fork at his head. Furio was quick though, and he caught it.

"Manners," Elena, the only female in the Guardians said in a sing-song voice.

"Only I can call him *blinky*," Fergie announced to end the argument, but Storm still didn't look happy.

Whatever. He would get over it. And if he didn't, then she could help him. Later. In bed.

"I would like to go over the contents of your laptop, after dinner perhaps?" Kingston asked.

"Well, sure, but it's no secret. L-Corp wanted as much research as they could get on old land surveys in Hudson, Bergen, and Essex counties. I'd only just begun, but I'd compiled some pretty extensive files with documents and references surrounding each of the GPS coordinates given to me. They took my computer each evening, and supposedly wiped it clean so I wouldn't have access after I handed it in, but I was able to save everything to my cloud before that so I have copies of everything they asked me to research."

"You saved all the information to your cloud? Like a corporate spy?" Storm said, and she was kind of miffed at his incredulity.

Fergie punched her mate in the arm and frowned

at the number of open-mouthed faces in the room. Only Jessenia winked.

"What because I like shoes and haven't been able to hold a job makes me a fucking idiot or something?"

"*No!*"

"*No.*"

"*Of course not.*"

She snorted and rolled her eyes. Fergie stood up from the table and placed her utensils in her now empty plate.

"Thank you, Keep!" she shouted, and the rest of them looked at her like she was certifiable.

"Just because the castle seems to magically prepare everyone's meals, and it automatically or magically cleans up after you all, doesn't mean it doesn't have feelings."

"Uh, love, the castle is an inanimate object," Storm began.

"Is it? Well, inanimate objects don't cook like this and they don't take suggestions from my friend there because I know that is her cauliflower recipe."

"That's true. I just kind of thought of it and here it was," Jessenia added, "who built this place anyway?"

Fergie waited for someone to answer the question, but they all simply looked at one or the other. Unbelievable.

"I can't believe that whatever magic you all are in the business of protecting, none of you ever thought to research the origins of the Keep's magic?"

The number of blank faces around the room answered that question. And they thought she was an idiot. Sigh.

"Whoever has my laptop should disable the GPS tracker before turning it on, but in the meantime here, I can give you access to my cloud, I just need your email address," Fergie picked up her cellphone and waited.

"Sure, send it to KBaldric001 at goc dot org," the Dragon said and cleared his throat.

"Done."

"Thank you, and can I say, uh, welcome as the first official *conpar* to an anointed Guardian of Chaos."

"But I thought you, *oof-*" Furio grunted from the fist Jessenia planted into his stomach.

The pained look in their leaders' eyes had every one of them frozen in place. Except for Fergie. She stepped forward, aware of Storm tensing at her movements. It was against Shifter decorum to touch someone else's mate, but she'd been a human first, so she figured she'd get a pass. Fergie opened her arms and hugged Kingston briefly dropping a platonic kiss on the man's cheek.

The lights in the room glowed brighter, warming them with its intensity for a brief moment, as if the Keep itself wanted in on the friendly gesture. Fergie stepped back, into the arms of her mate who'd stood when she did. He gripped her tighter than was necessary in her opinion, but she secretly liked it.

"Thank you, Kingston, I am honored."

"My *conpar*. Hmm. It is a bit formal, but I like it, *nushe*," Storm grinned.

Kingston nodded at her once, then stood to leave the room. Before he exited, he placed his big hand on the wall of the dining room and looked up at the ceiling with one eyebrow raised.

"Thank you, Keep," growled the most powerful Shifter amongst them, to the astonishment of everyone there.

Fergie just smiled.

Epilogue

Storm gazed at his mate in the light of the rising sun as it filtered into their bedroom through the new gauzy drapes she'd had him install. It was one of the several pleasant changes his sweet Fergie had made in his life and he couldn't help but be grateful for each of them.

"Love," he whispered and brushed his lips over her smooth cheek, tucking a stray behind her ear. "They're here, my love, wake up."

Fergie moaned and turned towards him. He couldn't really blame her. Poor thing. She was more than likely worn out from the exertion of the night before.

Together they'd run through the pine barrens in

their fur by the light of her first full moon as a Wolf Shifter. Her red fur had gleamed in the silvery light of that magnificent globe, and together they'd chased shadows and rabbits. They'd ventured to all the magical places nearby and partook in the cool, clean waters from the mystical *Blue Hole*. A favorite swimming spot for local supernaturals.

His mate was as beautiful and fierce in her Wolf as she was in her skin. Larger than their wild cousins, Wolf Shifters burned a lot of calories in their animal forms. He was thrilled to discover their telepathic abilities were strong in that shape as well.

Projecting his thoughts to his other Guardians was something Storm had gotten used to out of necessity but being in his mates head especially during lovemaking was positively thrilling. He'd never tried to talk in his fur before, but with her it was as natural as breathing.

He'd been so concerned about her transformation, he hadn't realized he was projecting until she'd responded inside his mind's eye.

I am fine. It did hurt, but it's okay now, love. Will you teach me how to run? Teach me to be a Wolf now, she'd pushed the thoughts into his mind and he'd welcomed both her voice and the challenge she presented.

Storm had never been much of a mentor to anyone, but Fergie was so full of life and curiosity. He'd shown her his favorite places and hidden trails. They'd spent hours wandering the forest. Then they'd returned home and slipped back into their skin. Afterwards, they'd made love and re-sealed their matebond by moonlight. It had been the best night of his life. Bar none.

"Mmm, what is it?" she asked

"Hello there, beautiful," he said and kissed her nose.

"Hello, yourself," she smiled and opened her arms, to which he eagerly went.

His mate was one hell of a *cuddler*. Who knew he'd grow to like that sort of thing? He never had before, but then again he'd never had a mate before. She wiggled closer and his body responded immediately and predictably.

"You asked me to wake you when they came, well, they came," he said and nipped her ear between his teeth.

"They're here?" Fergie yelped.

She practically toppled him over in her haste. He had to remember her new strength, but for now he'd just thank the gods for his own wolfish reflexes.

"Where? Where are they?" she pulled on a short

robe he found ridiculously sexy and pinched his arm impatiently.

"Ow," he frowned, "that hurt."

"I'm sorry," she said, and kissed his chin, her whiskey eyes sparkled mischievously.

"Come on, I can't wait either," Storm tugged her hand and walked her across the floor to the new door that had appeared in their room just after she'd moved in.

It seemed the Keep was happy with his little *nushe*. His *conpar*, he corrected himself though both terms of endearment were perfect for his Fergie.

He'd never heard the term *conpar* before, but now that he knew it meant 'beloved mate', it was the only way he thought of his sweet Fergie.

She squealed excitedly when he opened the door with flourish and he was glad he'd thought to add a few more surprises to her order. She deserved them. Especially after what he'd done to three pairs of her panties this week. Darn claws.

Who was he kidding? Storm loved it when his mate squealed with delight whenever he tore her panties from her sweet body.

"My lady," he bowed and grinned as Fergie entered their brand-new two-thousand square foot walk-in closet.

Technically, it was theirs, but he only took up a small part of the enormous space with his clothes and weapons. The rest was all hers.

"OH MY GAH! I love you so much," she jumped at him and kissed him hard on the mouth before leaping off to open her goodies.

Storm sat on the velvet chaise at the bottom of the spiral staircase that led to the second floor of the expansive room. Fergie gasped and awed at the bounty before her and joy filled him as he watched her open gifts like a child on Christmas.

"I am not a child," she mock scolded, "but I so enjoy presents. These are so beautiful and there are so many of them!"

"Fifteen pairs, and a few selections from the lingerie department," he nodded at the pink packages on the side of the mountain of shoes.

He was proud of his haul and anxious to see her wearing them. And nothing else, of course. Fergie dropped the box of the fourth pair she'd opened and leapt onto his lap. His hands closed around her bottom and he hugged her close, worried she'd fall and hurt herself.

"Don't you want to open the rest?"

"Not now, now I want my real present," she said and pressed her mouth to his.

"Fergie," he nibbled her lips unable to resist the sweet temptation she presented.

"I love you, you know, even without the shoes," she whispered and his heart pounded in time with hers.

"It makes me happy to make you happy," he returned squeezing and caressing her spectacular ass beneath the silky robe.

"I only need you for that, mate," she wiggled against him and he immediately rose to the occasion.

"Let's open the rest later," he said.

"Best idea you've had so far," Fergie agreed.

Damn, he loved her. And he would make it his business to show her. Again and again. He swallowed her moan as he began to exhibit the extent of his immeasurable feelings.

Sometime later...

Only fourteen pairs of luxury heels, including all six Louboutin's, had survived. One pair of Jimmy Choo's had unfortunately broken beneath his body. But, hell, was it worth it. He'd replace it later.

"Damn straight you will," his *conpar* moaned aloud.

Then she was speechless, and finally, she was gasping his name, which was coincidentally just how he liked her.

"Mine."

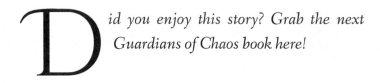

id you enjoy this story? Grab the next *Guardians of Chaos* book here!

P.S

Don't forget to tell me how you liked this story by leaving your honest review! *No pressure.* 😊

A review can be one or two brief sentences where you simply state whether you enjoyed the story and would recommend it to someone! It is an enormous help to authors and the best way for us to reach larger audiences so we can keep writing the stories you love!

Thank you so much!

Xoxo!

Del mare alla stella,

C.D. Gorri

Have you met my Dragons?

The Falk Clan Tales are my stories surrounding four Dragon Shifter brothers and how they find their one true mates.

Each brother's chest is marked with his rose, the magical link to his heart and his magic. They each have a matching gemstone to go with it.

She's given up on love, but he's just begun.

In *The Dragon's Valentine* we meet the eldest Falk brother, Callius. He is on a mission to find a Castle and his one true mate, one he can trust with his diamond rose....

His heart is frozen; can she change his mind about love?

In *The Dragon's Christmas Gift* our attention shifts to Alexsander, the youngest brother of the four. He has resigned himself to a life alone, until he meets *her*.

Some wounds run deep, can a Dragon's heart be unbroken?

The Dragon's Heart is the story of Edric Falk who has vowed never to love again, but that changes when he meets his feisty mate, Joselyn Curacao.

She just wants a little fun, he's looking for a lifetime.

We finally meet Nikolai Falk and his sexy Shifter mate in *The Dragon's Secret*.

*Now available in a boxed set.

Look for The Dragon's Treasure in 2022!

Connect with C.D. Gorri

To learn more about me please visit:
https://www.cdgorri.com
https://www.facebook.com/Cdgorribooks
https://twitter.com/cgor22
https://www.bookbub.com/authors/c-d-gorri

TikTok

Visit my website to find out more about my supernatural world also known as the Grazi Kelly Universe and sign up to be a subscriber!
https://www.cdgorri.com/newsletter

Have you met my Bears?

Looking for a Paranormal Romance series that is loads of growly fun?

Meet the Barvale Clan first in the Bear Claw Tales! A complete shifter romance series about 4 brothers who discover and need to win their fated mates!

Followed by two more spin off series, the Barvale Clan Tales and the Barvale Holiday Tales!

No cliffhangers. Steamy PNR fun. Go and read your next happily ever after today!

Other Titles by C.D. Gorri

Other Titles by C.D. Gorri

Young Adult Urban Fantasy Books:

Wolf Moon: A Grazi Kelly Novel Book 1

Hunter Moon: A Grazi Kelly Novel Book 2

Rebel Moon: A Grazi Kelly Novel Book 3

Winter Moon: A Grazi Kelly Novel Book 4

Chasing The Moon: A Grazi Kelly Short 5

Blood Moon: A Grazi Kelly Novel 6

*Get all 6 books NOW AVAILABLE IN A BOXED SET:

The Complete Grazi Kelly Novel Series

Casting Magic: The Angela Tanner Files 1

Keeping Magic: The Angela Tanner Files 2

G'Witches Magical Mysteries Series

Co-written with P. Mattern

G'Witches

G'Witches 2: The Hary Harbinger

Paranormal Romance Books:

Macconwood Pack Novel Series:

Charley's Christmas Wolf: A Macconwood Pack Novel 1

Cat's Howl: A Macconwood Pack Novel 2

Code Wolf: A Macconwood Pack Novel 3

The Witch and The Werewolf: A Macconwood Pack Novel 4

To Claim a Wolf: A Macconwood Pack Novel 5

Conall's Mate: A Macconwood Pack Novel 6

Her Solstice Wolf: A Macconwood Pack Novel 7

Also available in 2 boxed sets:

The Macconwood Pack Volume 1

The Macconwood Pack Volume 2

Macconwood Pack Tales Series:

Wolf Bride: The Story of Ailis and Eoghan A Macconwood Pack Tale 1

Summer Bite: A Macconwood Pack Tale 2

His Winter Mate: A Macconwood Pack Tale 3

Snow Angel: A Macconwood Pack Tale 4

Charley's Baby Surprise: A Macconwood Pack Tale 5

Home for the Howlidays: A Macconwood Pack Tale 6

A Silver Wedding: A Macconwood Pack Tale 7

Mine Furever: A Macconwood Pack Tale 8

A Furry Little Christmas: A Macconwood Pack Tale 9

Also available in two boxed sets:

The Macconwood Pack Tales Volume 1

Shifters Furever: The Macconwood Pack Tales Volume 2

The Falk Clan Tales:

The Dragon's Valentine: A Falk Clan Novel 1

The Dragon's Christmas Gift: A Falk Clan Novel 2

The Dragon's Heart: A Falk Clan Novel 3

The Dragon's Secret: A Falk Clan Novel 4

The Dragon's Treasure: A Falk Clan Novel 5

Dragon Mates: The Falk Clan Complete Series Boxed Set Books 1-4

The Bear Claw Tales:

Bearly Breathing: A Bear Claw Tale 1

Bearly There: A Bear Claw Tale 2

Bearly Tamed: A Bear Claw Tale 3

Bearly Mated: A Bear Claw Tale 4

Also available in a boxed set:

The Complete Bear Claw Tales (Books 1-4)

The Barvale Clan Tales:

Polar Opposites: The Barvale Clan Tales 1

Polar Outbreak: The Barvale Clan Tales 2

Polar Compound: A Barvale Clan Tale 3

Polar Curve: A Barvale Clan Tale 4

Barvale Holiday Tales:

A Bear For Christmas

Hers To Bear

Thank You Beary Much

Purely Paranormal Pleasures:

Marked by the Devil: Purely Paranormal Pleasures

Mated to the Dragon King: Purely Paranormal Pleasures

Claimed by the Demon: Purely Paranormal Pleasures

Christmas with a Devil, a Dragon King, & a Demon: Purely
Paranormal Pleasures (short story)

Vampire Lover: Purely Paranormal Pleasures

Grizzly Lover: Purely Paranormal Pleasures

Elvish Lover: Purely Paranormal Pleasures

Hot Dire Wolf Nights: Purely Paranormal Pleasures

Christmas With Her Chupacabra: Purely Paranormal
Pleasures

The Wardens of Terra:

Bound by Air: The Wardens of Terra Book 1

Star Kissed: A Wardens of Terra Short

Waterlocked: The Wardens of Terra Book 2

Moon Kissed: A Wardens of Terra Short

*Now in a boxed set and in audio!

The Maverick Pride Tales:

Purrfectly Mated: Paranormal Dating Agency: A Maverick Pride Tale 1

Purrfectly Kissed: Paranormal Dating Agency: A Maverick Pride Tale 2

Purrfectly Trapped: Paranormal Dating Agency: A Maverick Pride Tale 3

Purrfectly Caught: Paranormal Dating Agency: A Maverick Pride Tale 4

Purrfectly Naughty: Paranormal Dating Agency: A Maverick Pride Tale 5

Purrfectly Bound: Paranormal Dating Agency: A Maverick Pride Tale 6

Also available in 2 boxed sets:

The Maverick Pride Volume 1

The Maverick Pride Volume 2

Dire Wolf Mates:

Shake That Sass: Sassy Ever After: Dire Wolf Mates Book 1

Breaking Sass: Sassy Ever After: Dire Wolf Mates 2

Pinch of Sass: Sassy Ever After: Dire Wolf Mates 3

Also available in a boxed set:

Dire Wolf Mates Volume 1

Wyvern Protection Unit:

Trusting Her Protector

Tempting Her Protector

Tricking Her Protector

Standalones:

The Enforcer

Blood Song: A Sanguinem Council Book

EveL Worlds:

Chinchilla and the Devil: A FUCN'A BookSammi and the
Jersey Bull: A FUCN'A Book

The Guardians of Chaos:

Wolf Shield: Guardians of Chaos Book 1

Dragon Shield: Guardians of Chaos Book 2

Stallion Shield: Guardians of Chaos Book 3

Panther Shield: Guardians of Chaos 4

Howl's Romance

Mated to the Werewolf Next Door: A Howl's Romance

The Tiger King's Christmas Bride

Claiming His Virgin Mate: Howls Romance

Twice Mated Tales

Doubly Claimed

Doubly Bound

Doubly Tied

Hearts of Stone Series

Shifter Mountain: Hearts of Stone 1

Shifter City: Hearts of Stone 2

Accidentally Undead Series

Fangs For Nothin'

Moongate Island Tales

Moongate Island Mate

Mated in Hope Falls

Mated by Moonlight

Shifters Unleashed Boxed Sets

Check out these amazing anthologies where you can find
some of my books

and the works of other awesome authors!

Coming Soon:

Ash: Speed Dating with the Denizens of Hell

Hungry Like Her Wolf: Magic and Mayhem Universe

Shifter Village: Hearts of Stone 3

Midnight Magic Anthology (Water Witch)

Mouse and the Ball: A FUCN'A Book

Tiger Claimed

For Fangs Sake

Tiger Denied

Werewolf Fever: A Macconwood Pack Novel 8

Moongate Island Captive

Witch Shield: Guardians of Chaos 5

Sweet As Candy (as seen in Once Upon An Ever After)

Taming Magic: The Angela Tanner Files 3

Rituals & Runes Anthology (Air Witch)

.

Excerpt from Code Wolf

"Are you fuckin' with me?"

"No, Randall, I assure you I am not fuckin' with you," Rafe Maccon eased his immense frame back into his oversized, black leather chair and narrowed his ice blue eyes at his Third and one of his oldest friends. How long had he known the man sitting in front of him?

Randall had come to Maccon City when Rafe was about ten, he looked the same then as he did now. Tall at six foot three inches, muscular, and more than a little intimidating to the Wolves under him with his long beard and equally long dark brown hair.

Rafe, however, was the Alpha. He was more amused than intimidated by his surly friend.

"A vacation?! What the fuck am I gonna do on a vacation? Come on, Rafe, this is bullshit!"

The door to Rafe's private office flew open and in strolled a very happy, very pregnant Charley Maccon, Rafe's wife. The Alpha's eyes glowed as they landed on his positively glowing mate. She wore a long, flowy dress. The shade was a pale-yellow color that, Randall admitted to himself, looked damn good with her creamy complexion and curly dark hair.

Their Alpha Female was quite something. There wasn't a Wolf Guard in the place who wouldn't lay down his/her life for her.

"Well, maybe you should consider a vacation to be a relaxing experience, Randy," she dropped a kiss on Randall's cheek and walked past him, over to her husband whom she kissed full on the mouth.

The way his Alpha's eyes homed in on her when she opened the door was nothing compared to the hungry gaze that followed her across the room.

Randall had noticed it took a while for Rafe to get used to his mate's habit of greeting everyone with a kiss or hug. Wolves were protective of their mates, but Randall thought his Alpha was doing an exceedingly good job of hiding his tension. Werewolves did not share very well.

Charley; however, had stood firm. That was the way she was raised, and she wasn't going to change for any, how had she put it? Neanderthal brow-beating husband, regardless of how cute his ass was!

Randall had no direct knowledge if the "cute ass" statement was true or not. And he didn't want to know. He liked Charley though, had from the beginning. He was musically inclined and often took to one of the common rooms to strum his guitar or play a few keys on the piano.

Excerpt from Shifter Mountain
by C.D. Gorri

Keeton's Mountain Lion hissed angrily as he boarded the plane for the States. Three months on Moongate Island did nothing to repair his faith in people. Shifter or human, they pretty much sucked.

True, he was no longer being blackmailed by the sniveling cretin who'd been part of his last black ops assignment. Fucker had stepped on a landmine deep in the jungles of a place Keeton was not at liberty to name. Not even in his own head.

Fucking hell.

Yeah, it meant he could return home now, but to who? Keeton had no family waiting for him. His few friends were back on the island, but that was no place for his inner feline. The beast craved the hills and valleys of the New Jersey forests he called home.

He'd bought a hundred acres of forest off the beaten paths of New Jersey's Panther Mountains years ago. Even commissioned the building of a cabin deep in the woods. The design was environmentally conscientious and entirely sound. Two stories high, it had its own generators, additional solar paneling, and wind turbines for power, and indoor plumbing.

He wasn't an animal, for fuck's sake. But even if Keeton was going to avoid people, he didn't have to be uncomfortable doing it. Eyes closed, he sat seemingly at ease, but he was keeping tabs on every living thing around him on the plane.

Once a soldier, always a soldier, his two commanders, Callan McGregor and Landry Smyth, had said that often enough. Both men were Shifters, a unique Alpha and Omega pair who'd completed their Triad once they'd found their mate in Sage Freeman, a smart mouthed human female. That had been Keeton's cue to leave the island he'd called home for eighty-nine and a half days.

They hadn't kicked him out or anything. On the contrary. But he was restless and antsy. The island could no longer contain his need for isolation.

Memories of the disgust on Bruce Taylor's face when he'd seen Keeton lose control of his shift during a particularly bloody battle were forever ingrained in his brain. The human male had been a new recruit in the special ops task force where Keeton had served his country for the last five years in secret.

Dismantling dictatorships and stopping atrocities the likes of which he could hardly put a name to before they could ever see the light of day had been his job, and blackmail was his reward.

He'd kept the fact that he'd unwittingly told the secret about Shifters to the human from Callan and Landry until the night Bruce had died believing Keeton was the only one of his kind. The two men had investigated his claims, making sure that he never downloaded or emailed the proof he'd recorded with his phone the night Keeton lost control.

The half a million dollars he'd sent to Bruce's offshore bank was nothing. He didn't care about the money. It was simply the point of it all. The man had not trusted Keeton because of his dual nature. And he'd lost his life as a result.

"We need to stick to this route, Bruce," he growled at the human who'd become increasingly toxic to their two-man operation.

"Think I'm gonna trust a fucking animal. I'll go this way," the man argued.

After a few more minutes of trying to convince him, Keeton threw his hands up. His beast scratched at his skin, the animal sensing something was not right. The sounds of the explosion and Bruce's bitter cry rang in his ears, but he died before Keeton could ever hope to reach him.

It was his fault. He was the reason Bruce had died. After pledging his life to help save lives, he'd brought death instead.

Keeton was better off on his own.

Excerpt from Fangs For Nothin'
by C.D. Gorri

"Are you out of your mind?"

Xavier DuMont, Vampire and Prince of the Tenebris Clan out of DuMont, New Jersey, ran a hand over his face. It was almost five in the morning on Wednesday, and he was still going over the weekly requests and complaints.

He could not believe it. One after the other, he'd received dozens of requests for formal introductions for most of the eligible young females in the Clan by their parents or some family matchmaker or other. It was the 21st Century, and yet, the Vampires of the Tenebris Clan still thought he needed an arranged marriage to run things!

"No, Lucius, I assure you my mind is sound."

"How can you be thinking of going away? To some retreat? At this time of year! You know, the whole Clan is up in arms over the tax laws your father had set into motion before his demise. Some are questioning your right to rule. Then, there is still the matter of your mating—"

"Lucius, for the love of fuck! I know what is going on in my own Clan. I am even now revoking those tax laws, people will just have to be patient."

"And what about meeting with these young females? Maybe that will quell some of the unrest—"

"No! I am not inclined to take a mate at this time. My father's grave has barely begun to grow grass. There is no rush!"

"There is pressure though, sire," Lucius Redwing insisted.

He was Xavier's oldest and most reliable friend. At nearly three hundred years old, they'd known each other for a considerable length of time. Lucius had been his childhood companion when they'd fled France for the New World. After settling the town of DuMont, his father had not only been the most productive of the local normals, but he had taken over their branch of the Clan.

Breaking ties with the old regime, and establishing their own rule, the DuMonts had done exceedingly well. Of course, coming into the new century had been difficult for some, but Xavier was determined to do it, to breathe new life into the old-fashioned world of Vampires. He would see them succeed and blossom in this age that was simply exploding with technology.

"I know you have plans, sire. But the anxious mamas are already parading their daughters resumes as if they were applying for a job." Lucius grinned. He waved a manila envelope bursting with applications for audiences with him from the most prestigious Vampire families in all of DuMont.

"For fuck's sake, Luc. Get rid of them," Xavier growled, and ran a hand over his face.

"Now, now. Surely, you know enough not to disrespect tradition and courtesy. These families are your staunchest supporters. Without their aid, your ascension to leadership could be challenged. The right mate would stop all of that—"

"I will not be forced into this, Luc. If anyone wants to challenge me for the right to lead, then he or she can face me out in the open. Not hide behind some political game."

"But sire—"

"No. I will not be manipulated. You should know that of me, old friend."

"Yes. Of course." Lucius nodded, placing the hefty envelope on the corner of Xavier's desk.

Vampires did not always inherit the right to lead. Princes were not born but made. Wasn't that what his father had always said? And yet, royal blood flowed in his veins. And it was because of that blood —*his royal DuMont blood*—that so many hungry mamas yearned to tie one of their young to him for eternity.

Fortunately, Xavier had avoided them. He refused to be pressured to take any of the hungry misses for his mate, as of yet. But with his recent ascension, that pressure was now on full keel.

Shit and fuck.

"I've got an idea," Lucius said, thrusting a copy of *The Nightly News* at him.

"What is it, Luc? I am in no mood."

"Read there," his friend said, pointing at an article on the bottom left.

"A retreat? I haven't been on one of those since I was ninety."

"Yes, but remember the fun? I brought my *sheep* at the time, and you pouted because I wouldn't share her!"

"As I recall, she came quite willingly to my bed when summoned, Luc. Why do they still call them sheep? My gods, that is positively medieval!" he replied.

"In case normals see the newspaper, of course."

"Impossible. The Covens bespelled the paper to only go to supes."

"It has happened, Xavier. You know this as well as I."

"True. And Luc, I am sorry about Temple. That was your donor at the time, was it not?"

"Temple? Yes. Not to worry, sire. You always did woo the ladies without trying. Besides, now they have their own donors on hand. You do not need to bring one."

"You don't have to do that, you know."

"What?"

"Calling me sire."

"I do have to call you sire, *sire*. You are my Prince."

"Oh, do shut up. I am your friend, Luc. You've known me my entire life."

"Yes, sire."

"Luc," he growled his friend's name.

"Shall I make the arrangements then?"

"Fine. I will go to this retreat for the weekend if

only to shut you up. And to get away from all this." He indicated the pile of correspondence.

"Very good, sire."

Excerpt from The Enforcer by C.D. Gorri

The moon would soon be full. Isabeau looked at the night sky and pulled the hood of her ivory sweater up over her fiery red curls. She passed between the red and sugar maples, a few tall beech trees, and a lonely pine when a low growl sounded next to her. She reached out to touch the thick fur of the adult she-Wolf who walked beside her through the forest trail.

"It's okay Artemis, let's finish our rounds and get home."

As she walked around the perimeter of her land she chanted an ancient language that few would be able to identify fortifying the wards around her large animal sanctuary. That was what the mortals around her thought it was, and for the most part they were correct.

To them, Isabeau Rose had just arrived in town a few years ago with the deed to five-hundred acres of Northern New Jersey farmland. Within a few months, she'd transformed the abandoned horse farm and the woods around it into a series of habitats for wild animals that were injured or discarded. Creatures that needed a haven for rehabilitation.

She had a main house for herself that boasted ten-bedrooms and six-full baths, an indoor pool and spa, two stables, one for her horses, the other for more exotic wildlife, two large red barns, and a state of the art veterinary clinic on the grounds.

"Out late, aren't you?" Beau turned around to find the source of the unfamiliar voice. She lifted her hand to calm Artemis who was ready to pounce on the intruder.

"Who are you?" she demanded.

"The real question is what are you doing out here so late? Surely your wards don't need reinforcement at this time of night, not out in this quiet New Jersey forest, Sorceress Rose?" The dark stranger spoke with an unearthly calm to his voice that put Beau on edge.

This was no mere mortal. She used her keen

sight to see him despite the darkness and almost gasped aloud. His face was perfect, except for a thin silver scar that ran from his left eyebrow to his chin. His eyes blazed cerulean blue fringed with impossibly dark lashes. They were carefully masked to hide his emotions.

About the Author

C.D. Gorri is a USA Today Bestselling author of steamy paranormal romance and urban fantasy. She is the creator of the Grazi Kelly Universe.

Join her mailing list here: https://www. cdgorri.com/newsletter

An avid reader with a profound love for books and literature, when she is not writing or taking care of her family, she can usually be found with a book or tablet in hand. C.D. lives in her home state of New Jersey where many of her characters or stories are based. Her tales are fast paced yet detailed with satisfying conclusions.

If you enjoy powerful heroines and loyal heroes who face relatable problems in supernatural settings, journey into the Grazi Kelly Universe today. You will find sassy, curvy heroines and sexy, love-driven heroes who find their HEAs between the pages. Werewolves, Bears, Dragons, Tigers, Witches, Romani, Lynxes, Foxes, Thunderbirds, Vampires, and many more Shifters and supernatural creatures dwell within her worlds. The most important thing is every mate in this universe is fated, loyal, and true lovers always get their happily ever afters.

Want to know how it all began? Enter the Grazi Kelly Universe with Wolf Moon: A Grazi Kelly Novel or pick up Charley's Christmas Wolf and dive into the Macconwood Pack Novel Series today.

For a complete list of C.D. Gorri's books visit her website here:

https://www.cdgorri.com/complete-book-list/

Thank you and happy reading!

del mare alla stella,
    C.D. Gorri

Follow C.D. Gorri here:
    http://www.cdgorri.com
    https://www.facebook.com/Cdgorribooks

https://www.bookbub.com/authors/c-d-gorri

https://twitter.com/cgor22

https://instagram.com/cdgorri/

https://www.goodreads.com/cdgorri

https://www.tiktok.com/@cdgorriauthor